THE PAST IS A
FOREIGN
COUNTRY

THE PAST IS A
FOREIGN
COUNTRY

GIANRICO CAROFIGLIO

Translated by Howard Curtis

Copyright © Gianrico Carofiglio, 2006
English Translation Copyright © Howard Curtis, 2007

First published in the UK in 2007 in hardback by
Old Street Publishing Ltd, 28-32 Bowling Green Lane,
London EC1R 0BJ, UK
www.oldstreetpublishing.co.uk
First published in Italian by Rizzoli in 2004
as *Il passato è una terra straniera*

ISBN-13: 978-1-905847-51-8

10 9 8 7 6 5 4 3 2 1

Printed and bound in the UK by CPD, Wales

Translator's Note

I should like to thank the members of my Italian translation workshop at the July 2006 summer school of the British Centre for Literary Translation in Norwich – Johanna Bishop, Mary Ledgard, Veronica Lloyd, Neil Roper and Shaun Whiteside – for their contributions to the translation of the opening section of Part One, Chapter 3.

The version of poker described in *The Past is a Foreign Country* employs a 32-card deck from which the cards 2 to 6 have been excluded. Aces count low or high.

PART ONE

SHE'S ALONE, LEANING on the bar, drinking a fruit juice. There's a black leather bag on the floor by her feet, and for some reason that's the thing that really draws my attention.

She's staring so hard at me it's quite embarrassing. When our eyes meet, though, she turns away. A few moments later, she looks at me again. This sequence is repeated several times. I don't know her, and at first I wonder if she's really looking at me. I even have the impulse to check if there's anyone behind me, but I stop myself. There's nothing behind me but the wall – I know that perfectly well because this is where I sit almost every day.

She's finished her drink now. She places the empty glass on the bar, picks up the bag, and comes towards me. She has short dark hair, and the determined but not very spontaneous manner of someone who's spent a lot of time struggling with shyness. Or with something else, something worse than shyness.

She reaches my table. She stands there for a few moments, not saying a word, while I try to assume what I think is a suitable expression. Without much success, I think.

'You don't recognise me.'

It isn't a question, and she's right: I don't recognise her. I don't know her.

Then she says a name, and something else, and then, after a brief pause, asks if she can sit down. I say yes. Or perhaps I nod, or make a gesture with my hand to indicate the chair, I'm not sure which.

For how long I don't know, I say nothing. It's hard to know what to say. Until a few minutes earlier, I'd been having breakfast, as I do every morning, preparing myself for an ordinary day, and now all at once I'd been sucked into a vortex and had come out somewhere else.

In some strange, mysterious place.

A long way away.

THERE WERE FOUR of us around the table. A thin, sad-looking guy, a surveyor by profession, Francesco, myself, and the man whose apartment we were in. His name was Nicola, and he was a fat man of about thirty, who smoked a lot and had difficulty breathing. He kept making a rhythmical, unnerving sound through his blocked nose.

It was his turn to shuffle the cards and deal. He repeated his little trick of shuffling them and dividing them into two smaller decks which he held between his thumb and index finger, but he was tired, and he was nervous. Half an hour earlier he had been up nearly a million, but in three or four hands he had squandered almost all his winnings. Francesco was winning, I was more or less equal with him, and the surveyor was losing a lot. We were beginning the last hand of stud poker.

The fat man cut the cards and said, 'Five card stud.' He said it in the same tone of voice he'd used all evening. What he thought of as a professional tone. A good way to recognise an easy mark at a poker table is to see if they use a professional tone.

He dealt the first card face down and the second one face up. A professional gesture, as if to prove my point.

A ten for the surveyor, a queen for Francesco, a king for me. His own card was an ace.

'A hundred,' he said immediately, throwing an electric blue oval chip into the middle of the table, and moistening his upper lip with the tip of his tongue. We all played. The surveyor lit a cigarette. The fat man dealt again.

An eight, another queen, an eight, and a seven.

"Two hundred," Francesco said. The fat man flashed him a look of hatred, then also put two hundred in the pot. The surveyor folded. He had been losing all evening and couldn't wait for the chance to call it a night. I played.

A ten, a king, a ten. It was my turn and I said two hundred. The others played. We came to the last card. An eight for Francesco, a nine for me, another nine for the fat man.

'Last bets,' I said, and the fat man immediately bet the equivalent of what was in the pot. Three eights were already face up. Did he have a straight? I looked him in the face and saw that his lips were tense and dry. In the meantime, Francesco put down his cards, said he wasn't playing, and stood up for a moment as if to stretch his legs.

That meant that if I had more than a pair I could relax. The fat man didn't have a straight after all. There was no way he could have one: the fourth eight was the card Francesco had face down. So I asked for time. To think, I said, but in fact I only wanted to savour that intoxicating feeling you get when you're cheating at cards and are sure of winning.

'I have no choice, I have to see you,' I said after a minute, resignedly, like someone who's sure he's going to lose the hand, but has unfortunately been lured into it by a cleverer and luckier player. The fat man had two aces. I had three kings. That meant I won the pot, which was nearly three million lire – more than my father's monthly salary at the time.

By now the fat man was really pissed off. Obviously, he didn't like losing. But what made him furious was losing to a moron like me.

The surveyor won the next hand, but there was nothing in the pot except small change. Then it was Francesco's turn to deal. He shuffled as he usually did – impersonally – cut the cards and dealt.

First a card face down, and then one face up. A queen for me, a king for the fat man, a seven for the surveyor, an ace for himself.

'Two hundred. This is the hand where I recoup my losses.'

The fat man looked at him in disgust, as if to say, bloody amateur. He put down the two hundred. I played. The surveyor didn't.

The cards were turned over again. I was making an effort not to look at Francesco's hands, even though I knew I wouldn't see anything strange. And if I didn't the others certainly wouldn't. Another queen for me, another king for the fat man, another ace for himself.

'If you want to play those aces you have to pay. Three hundred.'

The fat man paid without a word, with the same look on his face as before. I thought about it for a while, touched the chips I had in front of me and then put down the money, looking unconvinced.

The fourth card. A ten for me, a jack for the fat man, a seven for Francesco.

'Another three hundred.'

'I'll see you,' I said.

'I'll raise you five hundred,' the fat man said in the same professional tone, moistening his upper lip and forcing himself to control his elation. The card he had face up was a jack. This was his hand, he was thinking. Both Francesco and I played. I looked like someone who thinks he's in over his head and is scared shitless.

The last card. Another ten for me, another jack for the fat man, a queen for Francesco. Angrily, Francesco passed. Obviously he couldn't play. He had thrown away a cool million. He said something to that effect but the fat man ignored him. He had a full house of jacks and kings, and was already enjoying his triumph. He was playing with amateurs, but he didn't care. He said he was betting the equivalent of the pot and lit a cigarette. What he was hoping was that my face-down card was another ten. If that was the case, then I would also have a full house. I would play and he would tear me apart. The idea that I might have the fourth queen in the pack was obviously something he had never even considered.

I saw him. My card was, indeed, the last queen. Which meant that my full house beat his. Abandoning his professional tone, he asked how the fuck something like that was possible.

We wrote it down on the sheet of paper where debts were recorded. According to that sheet, the big man was already bankrupt. Then we played for about another forty minutes, but nothing out of the ordinary happened. The surveyor won back a little, and the professional lost another few hundred thousand.

At the end of the game I was the only winner. Francesco gave me almost four hundred thousand lire, the surveyor wrote me a cheque for just over a million, and the fat man another cheque for eight million two hundred thousand.

The three of us got ready to leave. At the door, I assured them I was available for a return match. I smiled modestly as I said it, like a beginner who's won a lot of money and is trying to act appropriately. The fat man looked at me without saying a word. He owned a hardware store and at that moment, I'm sure, he'd have liked to smash my head in with a monkey wrench.

Once out in the street, we said goodbye and went our separate ways.

A quarter of an hour later, Francesco and I met up again at the railway station, in front of the bookstall, which was closed for the night. I gave him back his four hundred thousand and we went off to a fishermen's bar for a cappuccino.

'Did you hear the noise the fat guy was making?'

'What noise?'

'With his nose. It was unbearable. Fuck, can you imagine sleeping in the same room as him? He must snore like a pig.'

'As a matter of fact, his wife left him when they'd only been married for six months.'

'If he calls again, what do we do?'

'We go back, we let him win two or three hundred thousand lire and we say goodbye. Debt of honour paid, now fuck off.'

We finished our cappuccinos, went outside where the boats were moored, and lit cigarettes as the sky grew lighter. It was nearly time for bed. In a few hours I would go to the bank and cash the two cheques. Then we would share the winnings.

❖

Giulia and I had quarrelled the day before. She'd told me she couldn't carry on like this and maybe it was better if we split up.

She was trying to provoke a reaction. She wanted me to say no, it wasn't true, we were just having a little bit of a crisis, we'd get through it together, that kind of thing.

Instead, I told her I thought she was probably right. I had a slightly downhearted look on my face as I said it, because I thought that was the appropriate expression. I was sorry that she was sad, I felt slightly guilty, but all I wanted was for the conversation to be over so that I could leave. She looked at me, uncomprehending, and I looked back at her, but I was already miles away.

I'd been miles away for some time.

She started crying silently. I made some trite remark to soften the blow. I knew this must be painful for her.

When she finally got on her bicycle and rode away, the only thing I felt was relief.

I was twenty-two years old, and until a few months earlier nothing had ever happened in my life.

3

THERE'S A SONG by Eugenio Finardi about a guy called Samson. An ace on the pitch, and really handsome. Skin like bronze and eyes of jade. Looks like someone who's never been afraid.

Francesco Carducci to a T.

He had a reputation, both as a footballer – top goal scorer in the university championships – and as the idol of all the girls. Even, if truth be told, of a few bored mothers. That's what people said, anyway. He was two years older than me and was studying philosophy, but had fallen behind. I never knew how many exams he still had to take, whether he had chosen a dissertation topic, that kind of thing.

There was a lot I never knew about him.

Until one night during the Christmas break of 1988, we'd been merely casual acquaintances. A few friends in common, a few football matches, a quick hello if we met by chance in the street.

Until that night, during the Christmas break of 1988, our paths had barely crossed.

There was a party at the home of a girl called Alessandra, a lawyer's daughter. Her parents were away at a ski resort, and the big, elegant apartment was all hers. People were drinking, others chatting, a few were rolling joints in the corners. But most were playing cards. For a lot of people, the Christmas holidays meant an endless round of card games. For money.

There was a baccarat table in the big drawing room, while in the living room they were playing *chemin de fer*. In the rest of the apartment, like I said, people were smoking and drinking. No different from hundreds of similar occasions. All perfectly normal.

Then the world, or mine at least, suddenly speeded up. Like a spaceship in a cartoon or a sci-fi film that shoots up into the sky and disappears amongst the stars.

I'd blown a bit of cash at baccarat and then gone into the room where they were playing *chemin de fer*. Francesco was at the table. I'd have liked to join in, but I didn't have enough money. There were kids who came to these parties with rolls of banknotes and even chequebooks. But I only got three hundred thousand lire a month from my parents and earned a bit more by giving private Latin lessons. I was attracted to the idea of playing for high stakes – and winning, of course – but I couldn't afford it. Or didn't have the guts. Or probably both. So, more often than not, I just watched.

There were at least sixty people wandering around the apartment. Every now and again the doorbell would ring and more people would arrive, sometimes one by one, but more often in groups. Some were complete strangers, even to Alessandra. These parties worked by word of mouth. It was a common form of night-time entertainment over the Christmas break to go from party to party, sometimes gatecrashing ones you hadn't been invited to, eat and drink something, and then leave without a hello or goodbye. That was the way it worked and there was usually no problem. I'd done it quite a few times myself.

So that evening no one paid much attention to the three guys who were roaming through the apartment without even taking off their leather jackets. One of them came into the room where people were playing *chemin de fer*. He was short and stocky, with close-cropped hair and a mean, stolid expression.

He rapidly eyed me and the others who weren't in the game but were just standing around. He wasn't interested in any of us. He went closer to the table to get a better look at the players. He immediately spotted the object of his search, quickly left the room, and returned less than a minute later with the other two.

One of them looked like a copy of the first, on a larger scale: quite tall and solid, with the same close-cropped hair. Not the kind of guy you'd pick a fight with. The third was tall, thin and blond, quite good-looking but with something sick about his features or his expression. He was the one who opened the conversation. So to speak.

'You piece of shit!'

Everyone turned round. Including Francesco, who had his back to the door and hadn't noticed the three guys until that moment. We all looked at each other for a few seconds, trying to figure out who they were after.

Then Francesco stood up and said calmly to the blond guy, 'Don't do anything stupid. There are lots of people here.'

'You piece of shit. Come outside or we'll wreck the place.'

'Fine. Just let me get my jacket.'

Everyone was frozen, paralyzed with shock and fear. The people in the room, and others you could see standing in the corridor, behind the three guys. I was frozen too, thinking they were going to take him outside and beat him to a pulp. Maybe before they'd even got down the stairs. I felt humiliated. I remember thinking, in a bizarre flash of lucidity, that this was how it must feel when you were about to be raped.

Francesco had gone over to a sofa where all the coats were piled. I heard my voice emerging from my mouth of its own volition, as if it belonged to someone else.

'Hey, you, mind telling us what your fucking problem is?'

I don't know why I spoke. Francesco wasn't a friend of mine and for all I knew he could well have done something to deserve what these guys had in store for him. Maybe the feeling of humiliation was just too much to bear. Or maybe there was some other reason. Over the years I've given it different names. One of them is fate.

Everyone turned to look at me. The short, stolid-looking guy came closer. He came really close, stretching his neck and shoving his face up at mine. He came *too* close. I could smell the mint-flavoured gum on his breath.

'Mind your own fucking business, asshole, or we'll beat the shit out of you, too.'

He really had a way with words.

I moved the way I'd spoken. Somehow, it wasn't me doing it. I brought my head down hard, as if smacking a ball into a goal, and broke his nose.

He instantly started bleeding, so stunned that when I kneed him in the balls he didn't even react.

What happened next I only remember as a series of still pictures, with a few slow-motion clips thrown in. Francesco hitting the tallest guy with a chair. Cards flying round the room. A few people coming in from the corridor and launching themselves into the fray.

The strange thing is that I remember all this without sound, like some kind of surreal silent film. One of the images in this film is a lamp falling off a little table and smashing. Without a sound.

We threw the three of them out, and then a strange feeling of embarrassment fell over the apartment. Some people knew, or thought they knew, the reason for this ill-fated punitive expedition. In other words, they knew, or thought they knew, what Francesco had been up to.

What they didn't know, and couldn't begin to imagine, was where I fitted in. And especially how I could possibly have done what I did. They stood in little groups, talking about it, and lowered their voices or stopped speaking when I came near. I wandered from room to room, feeling ill at ease, but trying to put a brave face on it.

I thought I'd wait a while longer, and then leave.

Even I couldn't understand what I'd done or why I'd done it. I broke his nose, I was thinking. Damn it, I broke his nose. One part of me was astounded by the violence I'd been capable of, while another part felt a strange, shameful elation.

People started to disperse, silently. Obviously, the game hadn't started up again after the interruption. I could leave now, too, I thought. After all, I'd come alone.

I put my jacket on and looked for Alessandra, to say goodbye.

What to say? I wondered. Thanks for the lovely party, I particularly liked the unscheduled part, it gave me a chance to let off steam and satisfy my baser instincts. But maybe she wouldn't see the joke. Maybe she'd headbutt me herself.

'Shall we go?' It was Francesco, standing behind me. He also had his jacket on. He was smiling somewhat ironically, but there was something like admiration in his eyes, too.

I nodded. It was as simple as that. At that moment it seemed natural, even though we barely knew each other.

Maybe he'll tell me what it was I just stuck my nose in, I thought.

We both went to say goodbye to Alessandra, who looked at us strangely. Her eyes were saying a lot of things. I didn't know the two of you were friends. I knew you were trouble, Francesco – everyone knows that – but you, Giorgio, I never imagined you were just as much of an animal as he is. Jesus, there's blood on the floor. The blood of the man you headbutted like a hooligan.

What her eyes were saying above all was: get out of here, both of you, and don't show your faces here again until the next millennium.

So we left together. When we were out in the street, we looked round cautiously. Just in case the three guys were stubborn and vindictive enough to try and attack us after the thrashing they'd received.

'Thanks. It took guts to do what you did.'

I didn't say anything. It wasn't that I wanted to seem like a hard man. I really didn't know what to say.

We'd started walking.

'Are you on foot?' he asked.

'Yes, I don't live far.'

'I have a car. Maybe we could go for a drive, have a drink, and I'll tell you all about it. I think I owe you that.'

'OK.'

He had an old cream-coloured Citroën DS with a burgundy roof.

'So, what do you think that was all about? In your opinion, what did those assholes want?'

'I don't know. Obviously the blond guy was the one who was after you. The other two were his minders. Was it over a woman?'

'Yes. That blond guy's a bad loser. But I'd never have expected him to do something as stupid as that.' He paused, as if he'd just thought of something annoying. 'Do you mind if we go somewhere, just for half an hour?'

'No. Where?'

'I think I ought to make sure they don't do anything else stupid. I need to talk to a friend of mine. This place we're going, you can get a drink as well, if you're not worried about the time.'

I nodded, as if I knew what was going on and felt comfortable with it.

In fact, I didn't really know what he was talking about. I had a vague idea, just as I was vaguely aware that I was about to cross a threshold that night. Or maybe I'd already crossed it.

I took a deep breath, settled in my seat in the DS as it glided silently through the deserted streets, and half closed my eyes. Damn it, I thought, I didn't care. I wanted to go.

Wherever we were going, I was ready.

4

THE FORECOURT OF an old municipal housing estate.

We got out of the car and walked into one of the big blocks.

There was no lift. A thin guy was standing on the stairs between the first and second floor, leaning against the wall, smoking a cigarette. Francesco greeted him, and he replied with a nod and then jerked his head towards me, questioningly. Who was I?

'He's a friend.'

That seemed to be enough. We passed and climbed two more broad flights of stairs. We knocked at a door, and after a few seconds – someone was looking at us through the spyhole – the door was opened by a guy who looked like the older brother of the man on the stairs.

The interior of the apartment was really strange. A little hall on the right led to a very large room. In it, there was a bar counter, the kind you find sometimes in small hotels, a few tables and a few people sitting drinking and smoking. They seemed to be waiting for something. A record player was playing, at low volume, a scratchy copy of the soundtrack from the film *Cabaret*.

There was a small room on the left, leading to another one on the far side. Green baize tables and people playing cards.

Francesco led me into the room with the bar. 'Sit down, have a drink, I'll be right back.' And without waiting for a reply he went into the other room, walked across it, and disappeared from view. I sat down at the only free table. No one came to take my order, and there was no one behind the bar. So I sat there, doing nothing, sure that everyone was looking at me and wondering who I was and what I was doing there.

In actual fact, no one was taking the slightest notice of me. They were all talking among themselves, and every now and again one of them turned round to look towards the other room. They were almost all men. Surreptitiously, I started observing the only two women in the room. One was short and fat, with narrow eyes close together and a brutish expression. She was sitting with two nondescript-looking men, and she was the one doing all the talking, in a low voice and a tone of barely contained anger.

The other woman was a very attractive brunette – though she must have been at least fifteen years older than me. A woollen V-necked sweater gave a glimpse of cleavage. She was the only person in the room I'd have liked to notice me. But she seemed completely smitten with the guy next to her, who was wearing a jacket and tie and a solid gold watch.

I was fantasising about the brunette – not the kind of thoughts I could have discussed with my maiden aunts – when Francesco materialised on the chair opposite me.

'Emma.'

I jumped slightly. 'Sorry?'

'Her name is Emma. She's married to C.M., but they're separated. You know who C.M. is, don't you? The frozen food guy. Five million a month in alimony and a house on the Piazza Umberto. A bit touched up here and there, but quite a dish all the same. Didn't you get a drink?'

'I didn't see anyone–'

Francesco stood up, went behind the bar, and poured two glasses of whisky. He came back to the table and handed me one. Then we lit cigarettes.

'So, why did you do what you did tonight?'

17

'I don't know. I've never headbutted anyone in my life.'

'That's odd, then. The way you broke his nose looked very professional. Did someone teach you?'

Yes, someone had taught me.

When I was fourteen or fifteen my friends and I often hung out in a billiard hall close to where I lived. Most of the time, we played ping pong, or sometimes pocket billiards. The place didn't exactly attract a high class clientele, and once I said something I shouldn't to this guy who was already a criminal at the age of sixteen. I mean a professional criminal. Dealing drugs, stealing cars, that kind of thing. I never found out his name, but everyone called him – when he wasn't around – Stinky. Personal hygiene wasn't really his thing.

Naturally, he played me like a bongo, while my friends did nothing. I almost expected them to look away and whistle. Anyway, while I was taking the beating and trying to limit the damage, another man stepped in. He was a criminal too, and all of eighteen years old. He was bigger than the other guy and, what's more, he was well known for being a lot more dangerous.

His name was Feluccio. Feluccio the Big Man. He was into all sorts of dodgy business and kept order in the whole of the block where the billiard hall was located. Of course, his idea of order was a very personal one, but that's another subject. For some reason, he liked me.

He bought me a beer and gave me a dishcloth with ice in it for the bruises. He told me I couldn't just take the blows like that. I replied that I could, and I was still here to prove it, but he didn't catch my subtle humour. He was worried about what was going to happen to me out in the urban jungle and decided I should be his pupil. He'd developed his own system of unarmed combat. If he'd been born in the Far East, he might have become a great master. Instead, he was here, in Bari, and he was Feluccio the Big Man, the street brawl and football stadium bust-up champion of the Libertà neighbourhood.

18

In the little yard at the back of the billiard hall, Feluccio the Big Man taught me how to headbutt my opponent, how to knee him in the balls, how to slap him on the ear to deafen him, how to elbow him in the chin. He taught me how to bring down someone bigger than me, by simultaneously pulling him by the hair and kicking him on the inside of the knee.

I don't know how far we'd have gone if my teacher hadn't been arrested one day by the carabinieri for a robbery. That was the end of my apprenticeship in the art of street fighting.

'That's how I learned to headbutt. At least now I know it works.'

'It's a nice story,' Francesco said when I'd finished telling it.

'You're right, it's a nice story. What is this place?'

'Can't you see? It's a kind of casino. Illegal, obviously. This room is where people wait to play. The first room is for the smaller games. The other rooms,' he made a vague gesture with his hand, 'are where they play for serious money.'

He drank some of his whisky and rubbed his eyes.

'I talked to that friend of mine,' he said, making the same gesture with his hand. 'We can breathe easily now. Someone will pay a visit to our friends from tonight and explain that it's not a good idea to cause any more trouble. And that'll be it.'

'How is it that you know…these people?'

'I come here to play sometimes.'

At that moment, another group of people arrived. Three girls, more or less my age, and two men, much older. About forty at least, with Rolexes, expensive suits and faces to match. One of the girls looked long and hard at Francesco, as if trying to meet his eyes. It didn't work.

'I think it's time to go – unless you'd like to sit in on a few games.'

'No, no. Let's go.'

So we stood up and walked to the main door. Francesco made no move to pay for the whisky. I was about to say something, worried that some roughneck would follow us down the stairs and shoot us in the legs, as punishment. Then it occurred to me that Francesco knew what he was doing. Maybe he had an open tab in this dive – pardon, casino – and in the end I said nothing. The girl kept looking at Francesco as we left the room. We said goodbye to the guy at the door, and the one on the stairs, and walked back outside.

When we drew up outside my building, Francesco asked me if I fancied a game of poker one of these evenings. At the home of some friends, he hastened to add, noticing the look of hesitation in my eyes. I told him my phone number – he didn't write it down, just committed it to memory – and we shook hands and said goodnight.

He owed me one, he said through the lowered car window when I was already out of the car and fiddling with my key in the defective lock. By the time I turned, he'd gone.

I went straight to bed, and stayed awake until the dawn light started to filter through the cracks in the shutters.

5

I WAS A MODEL STUDENT. Last year of law, ahead with my exams, my thesis on criminal law almost finished, and with a near-perfect record in my assessments. I was due to graduate in June, and then I would decide what to do. Teach at university or take the exam to become a magistrate. All very straightforward, very neat and tidy.

I'd been with Giulia for nearly two years. She was a medical student, the same age as me. She wanted to be a doctor, like her dad. She was pretty and petite. Her mum liked me a lot. All my girlfriends' mothers had liked me.

Everything was going well.

◈

Francesco phoned me four or five days later. The New Year had come and gone, and it was already 1989.

Did I still fancy a game of poker? Yes, I did. So we made an appointment for ten that evening, at the apartment of someone I didn't know. He gave me the name and address and I said I'd be there.

At nine I quarrelled with Giulia – our first real quarrel since we'd been together, but not the last – and by ten I was at the address Francesco had given me.

I'd brought five hundred thousand lire with me, which for me was quite a lot. I didn't want to look poor.

The other people there besides Francesco were the owner of the apartment – a fair-haired guy with long, oily hair, named Roberto – and a rather dirty-looking man of about forty. He introduced himself only by his surname – Massaro – and for the whole evening no one called him by his first name.

It was a shabby apartment. The furniture was of poor quality, and naked bulbs hung from the ceiling.

We played in the kitchen. The fair-haired guy put a bottle of whisky and two plastic cups next to the sink. He said we could help ourselves, which we did many times during the course of the evening, until the bottle was empty. Only Francesco drank hardly anything.

We started playing. The custom of the house was to play three hands of draw poker to one of stud poker. There was a fixed stake of ten thousand lire and a limit to how high the pot could go. The game was obviously out of my league. But I was ashamed to leave, so I started losing, a little at a time. I'd put in my stake, maybe make the first bet, then they'd up the ante and I'd have to fold because I was afraid of losing everything in a single hand. I did win a couple of small pots but after playing for about two hours I had almost nothing left and was cursing my own stupidity. Then something happened.

It was time to play stud poker, and Francesco dealt. One card face down, then one card face up. My face-up card was a queen, and so was my face-down card. The fair-haired guy had a ten, Massaro a king, Francesco an ace.

'Fifty,' Francesco said. The other two played immediately. I thought about it for a few seconds – I had just over a hundred thousand lire left – and then told myself, what the hell, I would lose the rest of my money, call it a day and never play again in my life. It would be a lesson to me.

Again, Francesco turned over the cards. I had the third queen.

I felt my heart racing. The fair-haired guy got another ten, and Massaro a jack. Francesco got another ace, so the choice was his.

'Two hundred thousand.' In other words, everything in the pot and more than I had left.

Damn, damn, damn, what do I do? The host played, Massaro said he was folding, and I said I didn't have all the money. Would there be any problem about giving me credit? No, Francesco said, no problem. The other man nodded. He probably didn't trust me, but didn't know how to say it. I put everything I had left in the middle of the table and we wrote down on a sheet of paper how much I owed the pot. Then Francesco dealt, for the penultimate time. An ace of hearts for me, a third ten for the fair-haired guy. A seven for Francesco.

'Five hundred thousand,' the fair-haired guy said.

Francesco passed, and I said I had to think. In fact I was genuinely terrified, and was trying to figure out what to do. What if his face-down card was the fourth ten? I had savings in the bank, but it seemed like madness to throw them away like this. Why the hell had I come? Why? I looked around and for a moment met Francesco's eyes.

He moved his head imperceptibly, as if telling me to play. I immediately looked away, afraid the others had noticed. They hadn't, so I played, writing down the vast amount I owed on the sheet of paper.

The last two cards slid across the table. A king for the fair-haired guy.

The fourth queen for me.

I was sure I could hear my heart beating wildly. Damn, I had four queens, which meant I was sure to have won. I prayed that the fair-haired guy's face-down card was the fourth ten, or at least a king. Because then he would play, come what may, and I would win. I felt as if I was going mad with the effort I was making to control myself.

I felt as if a drug was coursing through my veins. I felt as if I was having an endless orgasm.

'It's up to the man with the three queens,' the fair-haired guy said. From the way he said it, I was sure he had either four tens or a full house. That meant he was certain he was going to win, going to tear me apart.

'One million lire.' The words, as I said them, sounded unreal, first in my mouth and then in the smoky, almost palpable air of that kitchen. What was a million? It was an unreal entity. At least it had been an unreal entity up until a few minutes earlier, but now it was being transformed into something concrete. Something that could be multiplied.

'Do you have the money?' the host asked, with a hint of contempt in his voice.

I felt the blood rushing to my cheeks. I was ashamed and angry because they were treating me like a pauper. I was also scared stiff that he would try to stop me playing because I didn't have the money. I made an effort to keep my voice under control.

'I don't have it here. I already said.'

'Sign an IOU.'

'If I lose, of course I'll sign an IOU.' What about you? I'd have liked to add. If you lose, will you give me cash or a cheque? But I didn't say anything, for fear he might be alarmed and not play.

'All right. A million, and I'll raise you another million.' The asshole was absolutely sure he was going to win, with his four tens. I didn't say immediately that I'd see him. After his last bet I'd become calm suddenly. I felt a kind of tranquil but fierce elation. I wanted to enjoy that feeling for a few moments. I looked around and thought I caught a very slight smile on Francesco's lips.

'I'll see you,' I said finally.

'I have the fourth ten under here. So unless you have the fourth queen...'

I turned over the card. 'Yes, I do have the fourth queen.'

He froze, staring at the card I'd turned over. He couldn't believe it. It wasn't possible for two fours to be dealt in a single hand of stud poker.

I couldn't believe it myself.

'Good hand,' Francesco said cheerfully, and the man turned to him with a look of genuine hatred. My own expression was seraphic. I was wondering how he would pay me all that money. I took what was in the pot and we wrote down on the sheet of paper what he owed me. It was a huge amount, and I had only his word for it that he'd be able to pay me.

By the time it came to play or sit the hand out, the fair-haired guy had won back a little, but was still losing millions. I was practically the only one winning. I thought it was the decent thing to say that I didn't mind carrying on. Before Roberto could say anything, Francesco intervened. He was sorry, he couldn't stay late, he had an appointment in the morning. So we had to stop, because obviously we couldn't continue with just three players.

The fair-haired guy wrote me a cheque for three million seven hundred thousand, Francesco gave me two hundred thousand in cash. Massaro gave me more or less the same amount.

As we were about to leave, being a polite young man, I thanked them for their hospitality and, as I said it, I realised it was the wrong thing to say. As if I'd not only won all that money but also wanted to take the piss out of them.

Though, come to think of it, maybe I *was* trying to take the piss out of them.

Roberto didn't say anything. Neither did Massaro, but he'd hardly said a word all evening. Both looked pale. They couldn't seem to get over what had happened. Francesco said he'd arrange a return match and we left together.

It was two o'clock in the morning, and I was sure I wouldn't find it easy to get to sleep. So when Francesco asked me if I wanted to go for a drink, I said yes. And as I'd won all that money, I ought to pay.

Yes, he said, smiling strangely, I ought to pay.

6

WE WENT TO a piano bar called the Dirty Moon, where they had live music and stayed open until dawn. We got cappuccinos and hot Nutella croissants straight from the bakery, and sat down at a table at the back.

'It was your night, eh?' Francesco said, with a curious tone to his voice that I couldn't quite figure out.

'Absolutely. Nothing like that'll ever happen to me again. Can you imagine? Two hands of fours in a game of stud poker. And I had the better of the two.'

'Why shouldn't it happen again?'

'Well…I don't think you can repeat a stroke of luck like that.'

'You know, life is full of surprises,' he said in a vague kind of way and with a strange expression on his face. Then he stood up, went to the bar and came back with a pack of French cards. He removed the cards up to the six, shuffled them and started dealing them as if there were four of us at the table and we were going to play poker. When I had five cards face down in front of me, he asked me to look at them.

'What do you mean?'

'Look at your cards. Let's pretend we're playing another hand.'

I looked at them. Four queens and an ace of hearts. I was dumb-struck. He turned over the cards he had dealt the other imaginary players. One of these ghosts had four tens.

I looked around. 'What...what the hell's going on?' I whispered, almost stammering.

'Luck is a fickle thing. It's flexible. It's even capable of favouritism if you ask it nicely.'

'Are you telling me you cheated tonight?'

'I don't like the word cheating. Let's say...'

'Let's say what? What the hell are you talking about? Are you telling me I won all that money because you cheated?'

'I helped you. You had the balls to continue playing, even though it was risky. It was a kind of experiment.'

'Are you telling me you cheated as an experiment and because of that I have four million lire in my pocket? Is that what you're telling me? You must be crazy. You involved me in a fraud. You involved me in a fucking fraud, damn it. And without even telling me. Damn it, I'd have liked to decide for myself if I wanted to turn into a cheat all of a sudden.'

I hadn't raised my voice, but I was angry. He didn't react, didn't lose his composure. But he did lose the ironic smile that had been hovering on his lips and assumed a serious expression. An *honest* expression. I know it seems absurd, but that's what I thought at the time.

'I'm sorry. I should have told you where that money came from. I mean: how you made it. If you think it's immoral, you can return the cheque, or simply not cash it. You have that cheque because we cheated, it's true, so if you don't want to have anything to do with cheating, take it out of your wallet and tear it up. It's entirely up to you.'

I was stunned. In my moral outrage I hadn't considered the possibility that I could give back the money. Or simply destroy the cheque and with it the proceeds of our foul deed. He was right, I could do what he said. But damn it, that money was *mine* now. The boot was on the other foot. I was trying desperately to find something to say, without success, when he spoke again.

'So that you have all the facts you need to make up your mind, there's one more thing you should know. Those two guys – Roberto and Massaro – are card sharks.'

'How do you mean?'

'Oh, they're strictly small time. The fair-haired one can only do one trick. When we're playing stud poker and it's his turn to deal, he knows which cards are face down. To do that trick, you mustn't cut the cards. Massaro was on his right. Sometimes he didn't cut, sometimes he lifted a small pack and then Roberto put the cards back exactly where they were before.'

I was flabbergasted. I hadn't noticed a thing.

Francesco continued with his explanation. 'They also have a system of signals for communicating with each other during the game. I don't know if you're following me.'

I was following. I was following, and how.

'They're a couple of lowlifes, but they've ruined quite a few people with this system of theirs. So now you know everything, and you can decide freely.'

That certainly put the matter in a new light, I thought. It was no longer a simple fraud on two unwitting but honest men who occasionally gambled. It was a genuine act of justice, and I wasn't the accomplice of a cheat, but the companion of Robin Hood.

Which meant I could keep the money.

Then it occurred to me that maybe I should share it with Francesco.

'If I decide to keep it,' I said cautiously, 'shall we share?'

He roared with laughter. 'I certainly think so. You're doing the right thing, friend. We've taken the money from a couple of real bastards. It's as if we'd robbed a drug dealer.'

For all I knew, I thought at that moment, Francesco may well have robbed a few drug dealers in his time.

'How did you do it?'

'I know a few tricks.'

'I gathered that. I want to know *how*.'

'Did you ever hear of a magician explaining his tricks? It isn't done, it's against professional ethics.'

He smiled in amusement and paused for a few moments.

'I was taught by a magician,' he resumed. 'He was a friend of my father's. When I was a child and we had a party, if we asked him he'd do these incredible tricks. I was obsessed with the idea of learning those tricks, and whenever anyone asked me what I wanted to be when I grew up, I said a magician. At ten I bought myself a manual with money I'd saved. And I started spending lots of time practising. When I was about fifteen – I remember it as if it was yesterday, my father had just died – I went to see the magician and asked him to teach me. I showed him what I'd learned on my own and he was impressed. He said I had talent. So two or three times a week for more than a year, I went to his place and had lessons. He said I had it in me to become a great magician. He said I'd be good enough to go on the stage.'

He stopped to light a cigarette. He had a faraway, nostalgic look in his eyes.

'Then he had a stroke.'

He fell silent. As if someone else had spoken and given him the news that his teacher had had a stroke. I also took out a cigarette and waited for him to start speaking again.

'He didn't die, but after that he couldn't do magic any more. And he stopped teaching me as well. A few months later I cheated at cards for the first time.'

'Why?'

'Why do I cheat? Or why did I cheat that first time?'

'Both.'

'I've often asked myself that, and I'm not sure I know the answer. Maybe I was angry because I knew I couldn't be a magician. Maybe I was angry with him for having a stroke before he'd taught me everything. I guess I was also angry with myself, because I didn't have the courage to drop everything and go away, find another teacher. But I was only sixteen at the time.'

He paused again and stubbed out his cigarette in the ashtray.

'Or maybe I was just destined for it. I mean, playing tricks at the gambling table is fun. It's a kind of skill, like doing tricks on a stage.'

'You're forgetting one small detail. If I go and see a show by a magician, I pay to be tricked. That's the contract between me and the magician. I buy the ticket and he sells me a trick, and I'm fine with that. If I sit down to play cards with a cheat and I think I'm playing a normal game…'

'You're right. But real life is always more complex than any examples we can think of. You just have to think about what happened tonight. They're waiting in that apartment like two spiders in a web, ready to tear their victims to pieces. They deserve what happened to them. There's nothing immoral about doing what we did.'

'But it's a crime,' I said, though I wasn't angry or aggressive any more. I had no desire to argue with him.

'True, it's a crime. But the only laws I personally feel bound not to violate are those that coincide with my own ethics. The other night, at Alessandra's, you smashed that Neanderthal's face. You committed a crime…'

'No. That was self defence.'

'In a general sense, yes, it was self defence, though from a strictly legal point of view you were the aggressor. He hadn't lifted a finger. But it was a morally justified act, just as it's morally justified to steal from thieves. And it's morally justified, in fact it's a duty to oneself, not to get cheated.'

'So, if I'm following you correctly, you've only ever cheated other cheats.'

'I didn't say that. But I do think if you're going to cheat, it must be justified by a moral defect of the person you're cheating. I'm sorry if that sounds exaggerated. The fact is, I don't cheat the poor, I don't cheat those who only play for enjoyment, and I don't cheat my friends.'

'So who do you cheat?'

'Bad people. In my opinion, taking money – cheating at cards – from morally reprehensible people is a kind of practical metaphor for justice.'

Then he paused, looked at me very seriously, and a moment later burst out laughing.

'All right, I am exaggerating a bit. One of the things I like most about this work is the actual fact of stealing. You saw for yourself, it's great fun.'

In the course of a few minutes everything had changed, and things I would have made cut and dried judgements about an hour earlier had become debatable at the very least. I realised, with a mixture of amusement and anxiety, that it was true: the way that money had come to me was actually *fun*.

I was starting to question everything, and it was like flashing a torch into the most hidden recesses of my mind.

If I could have turned the clock back four or five hours, to before the game had started, would I still have played, knowing what was going to happen? And having the power now, after the fact, to decide that the money had come to me legitimately rather than through fraud, what should I do? Giving back the cheque or at least not cashing it: I wasn't thinking about that any more. I was already beyond that, well beyond that. And I answered my own questions. Everything was fine, I would have played anyway, even if I'd known what was going to happen. And it was much more fun getting that money as the result of a card trick – in other words, because of superior skill and human intention – than as the result of some banal piece of luck.

And then I realised something unsettling. More unsettling than all the rest of it.

I wanted to do it again.

Francesco read my thoughts. 'Do you fancy another game, in a few days' time? Fifty-fifty?'

'Let me ask you something. Why do you need me?'

He explained why he needed me. You can't cheat alone, especially at poker. If you're playing for serious money and you always win – and win a lot – when you're the one dealing the cards, the others soon notice and become suspicious. The assistant is just as important as the magician. One fiddles the cards, the other cashes in and everyone's happy. Well, not exactly happy, but they think it's just their stupid bad luck. Like Roberto and Massaro.

Briefly, Francesco showed me how it worked. At the table, the assistant has to act like an idiot or a show-off, which in poker amounts to the same thing. He can either have one big win or several small wins, depending on the game. The magician himself has to lose a bit, and the assistant's victory should look like a classic case of beginner's luck. And so on.

When he'd finished, I asked the question I was burning to ask. 'Why me?'

He looked at me in silence. Then he looked away, took out a cigarette and tapped it on the table, without lighting it. Then he looked at me again, still in silence. When at last he spoke, he seemed slightly ill at ease.

'I don't usually trust my intuition. In fact, I try to disregard it. But in your case, I had an intuition that you were the right person, someone who could *understand*. Have you ever read *Demian*?'

I nodded. Yes, I had read it, and if he was trying to convince me he'd hit the right note. But I didn't say anything.

'In other words,' he continued, 'I did something I don't usually do. I took a chance based on an intuition. Do you understand what

33

I'm saying?'

He was saying that he trusted me. Because of something special that *I* had.

That was enough for me.

Of course it was obvious he'd had another assistant before me. I was replacing someone. But Francesco didn't talk about it, and I didn't ask him about it that night.

By the time we left the Dirty Moon, the barman and the only waiter left were starting to put the chairs on the tables.

Outside, a pale January dawn was breaking.

7

I WENT TO Giulia's almost every evening. When I finished studying, or when the whole day had gone by and I hadn't managed to get anything done. That was something that happened occasionally, and when it did, I always felt slightly but unpleasantly frantic. It was like a physical sensation, a tingling in my arms and shoulders. I would become annoyingly aware of the clothes on my body, my breathing, my heart beating slightly faster than usual.

I'd go out, and knowing that I had an aim as I walked through the city would make me feel a little less anxious.

Giulia was always at home, studying with her friend Alessia. They were very alike, Giulia and Alessia. Both good students from well-to-do professional families, both used to a comfortable, settled existence. Apartments in the centre of Bari, furnished with expensive furniture from the Seventies, villas in Rosa Marina, skiing holidays, games at the tennis club, all that kind of thing. I was like a foreign traveller in that world, lost but curious. My own family came from a different territory entirely. The Party, politics, contempt for that opulent, parasitical section of Bari society. The proud, slightly snobbish sense of being a minority, and wanting to remain one. Even my sister was like that.

I, on the other hand, had always been curious about that other world. And mixed in with the curiosity was a kind of envy. For a life that seemed easier, less problematic, one in which you weren't constantly, obsessively criticising everything.

So when I started going out with Giulia I really began to explore that world.

I liked going into these people's homes, and seeing the lives they led, joining in their rituals, being with them without ever really being part of them. I was playing a game, a game of pretence, of mimicry. It was amusing for a few months, as long as it took me to get a fix on things.

At the time this story starts, I was already tired of the game, though I hadn't yet realised it.

I would go to Giulia's, and she and Alessia would stop studying. We'd hang out in the big kitchen, chatting away. Her mother would come in from her afternoon excursions to the shops, boutiques, hairdressers, beauty parlours, and she'd often stay and chat. Until she realised she was late for something. A game of burraco, a dinner, the theatre, whatever. She went out practically every evening. We almost never saw Giulia's father. He'd stay late in the apartment next door, where he had his surgery and spent all his time.

We often spent all evening in the apartment. Sometimes alone, just Giulia and I. Or sometimes friends would come over – her friends – and we'd make spaghetti or salad. It was mainly at weekends that we all went out together, to the cinema or a pizzeria.

I don't remember what we talked about all those evenings in the kitchen of the De Cesare apartment, among the rows of pans hanging as if on display, immersed in that clear light and that clean, comfortable smell. A smell of home and fresh food and expensive soap and leather.

That was what I liked most when I arrived there: to smell that nice, reassuring smell. And sometimes I wondered what people smelled when they entered my home, and what that smell – which I was no longer aware of – told them about my family.

The evening after the poker game with Roberto and Massaro, I got to Giulia's a little earlier than usual. I'd cashed my share of the winnings that morning, and I'd bought her a bag. In order to beg her forgiveness for the previous evening's quarrel, and to quell my own vague sense of guilt.

I gave her the gift and she opened it, looking rather surprised. When she saw what it was, she looked at me, even more surprised, because it was an expensive bag and there was no reason for such a big gift.

'I wish I had a boyfriend like that,' Alessia sighed as she left.

When we were alone, I told Giulia what had happened. The part I could tell her, obviously. I'd played some poker, and I'd been incredibly lucky and won a lot of money. That was more or less it.

'*How* much did you win?' Giulia asked, wide-eyed, moving her head closer to mine. As if to make sure she'd understood.

'A few million lire, I told you.' Instinctively, I realised it was better to keep it vague.

'A few million. Have you gone crazy? Where did you play?'

She wasn't angry. She was astonished, incredulous.

'At the home of a…a friend of Francesco Carducci's.'

'Ah, you're really a friend of Francesco Carducci's now, aren't you? First you get into a fight together, then you go gambling with him. What next? Are you going to be off chasing skirts with him? Should I tell my mother to be careful when you're around?'

'He invited me because they needed a fourth player. I told you yesterday, when you got angry.'

'You didn't tell me *who* had invited you.'

'Well, as you see, I had nothing to hide. For a while it was a perfectly normal game. Then there was this incredible hand, with two fours dealt. I didn't do anything to push the game in a particular direction, that's just the way it worked out.'

As I spoke, it struck me very clearly that my life was splitting into two halves. One half was normal and the other had moved into a shadowy area I couldn't talk to anyone about. At that moment I knew I'd started leading a double life.

And I liked the idea.

'What I don't understand is how the two of you ever became friends.'

'We haven't become *friends*. Not that there'd be anything bad or strange about it if we had.' I was aware of a curious tension in my voice as I said this, as if I had to defend Francesco from the prejudice implicit in Giulia's words. And even at that moment, I realised, I wasn't being honest with her. I really had become a friend of Francesco's, and I wanted him to become my friend.

'That night when we got into a fight at Alessandra's, we left together. After what had happened, it seemed quite natural. When we said goodnight, we agreed to meet again some time. Then he was missing a fourth at poker and he called me. That's all.'

'And what if, instead of winning all that money, you'd lost it?'

'There was no way I could have lost that hand, not with four queens.' It was the truth, I told myself. I was just leaving out a few details.

Giulia was silent a while. Then she picked up the bag again, turned it around in her hands, and tried putting it over her shoulder. 'It's beautiful.'

I nodded, and smiled like an idiot.

Finally, she put the bag aside, and asked me if she ought to be worried: you know what they say about people who are lucky at cards. I said I didn't think there was anything to worry about, but if she liked, we could check. As long as we had a little privacy. Well, we had privacy all right, given that her sister had been married for six months, her father was away at a conference somewhere, and her mother was out playing burraco. Just for a change.

We made love in her room, and I was strangely conscious of all my movements and gestures. Even the most insignificant. It was disturbing, how much I felt in control. I was aware of being there, as our bodies moved together in a way they'd never moved before, and simultaneously of being somewhere else.

We lay side by side in her bed and Giulia said that if winning at poker had that effect on me, well, she was willing to let me play a few more times. I didn't say anything.

I was looking up at the ceiling. I was alone in the room.

8

AT LEAST TWO weeks had passed, and Francesco hadn't called me again. After a few days I'd become convinced that he'd had second thoughts, that he'd realised he'd made a mistake and had decided to drop me. Quite rightly.

I'd thought of calling him myself, but hadn't. I didn't want him to see how tempted I'd been by his proposal. I didn't want to admit it even to myself. I told myself it was better this way. My life resumed its sluggish course.

One Friday afternoon, as I was trying to apply myself to the manual of civil procedure, the call came. When I heard his voice, I had a rush of adrenalin. He didn't tell me why he hadn't phoned before and I didn't ask him. Did I fancy going out that evening? I said yes, thinking about what I could possibly tell Giulia. Obviously I'd have to make something up.

'All right,' he said, 'I'll pick you up about ten. We're going outside Bari.'

'Where?'

'To a party.'

As it turned out, Giulia wasn't a problem. She'd gone down with flu and when I called her she herself told me it was better I didn't come over tonight if I didn't want to get ill myself. All right, I said, trying to sound disappointed. In that case, I might go out for a drink with some friends – my friends – just to pass the time.

The reason I said this was to avoid her calling me at home when

I was already out with Francesco. The next day I'd think of something to tell her.

❖

Francesco was punctual. When I left the building he was already waiting outside, double parked in his DS. He had a smile on his face, a smile I'd soon learn to recognise but would never really manage to figure out.

We sped through the half-empty streets. In a few minutes, we were out of the city. It was a cold, clear night. The moon was full, and the countryside gliding past us was bathed in a magical pale blue light. You didn't need headlights, you could go anywhere on a night like this.

We hardly spoke. Silence usually made me anxious, and I spoke to fill the void, but not that night. That night I felt calm but excited, a kind of tingling inside me. Like being slightly drunk but also completely in control. I didn't need to speak.

We turned into an avenue lined with tall pines. The grounds beyond them were like a forest. There was a villa at the end of the avenue, and on the right an open space where a number of cars were parked, most of them shiny and expensive. We parked there, too, and climbed a wide flight of steps to the house.

'Whose party is this?' I asked, having just realised I had no idea.

'A girl named Patrizia. Her father's a millionaire. They have hundreds and hundreds of hectares of wheatfields, among other things. It was her birthday a few days ago, I think.'

I was about to say something about the fact that we'd come empty-handed, then it occurred to me that it was his problem, if it was a problem at all.

Behind the glass-paned door there was a wide entrance hall. From there we passed into a very large reception room.

41

The room was in semi-darkness. The chandelier in the middle of the ceiling was off and the dim lighting came from hidden floor-level lights.

It was hot. There were a lot of people here, some our age and others older. Quite a few over forty. The room smelled of cigarettes, perfume on warm bodies, wax furniture polish. There was something tangible in the air, something physical, carnal.

Francesco said hello to a few people and looked around for the hostess. A girl approached him from behind, took him by the shoulders, turned him round and gave him a big hug. 'You came! I'm so glad.'

'Why? Is there any reason I shouldn't have come?'

I thought I caught a sardonic tone in his voice. Or maybe I imagined it. It didn't matter at that moment.

'This is my friend Giorgio. Giorgio, meet Patrizia, one of the most dangerous women in the region. She's a Judo champion.'

She turned to me and seemed really pleased to meet me: Francesco's friend. I didn't know how to react: giving her my hand seemed clumsy, bureaucratic. She solved my dilemma by giving me a hug and kissing me, as if we'd known each other for ages. She was fairly short and solid, with brown hair, dark, slightly wild eyes, and a wide, masculine nose. She conveyed a sense of physical vigour, a cheerful, down-to-earth sensuality. My thoughts had started off along their usual track. I wondered how she would look naked, what it would be like to fuck her. I imagined a white, muscular body against the wall, and me taking her roughly, from behind. Hooray for Judo.

'And are you a bandit like him?' she asked, cheerfully. 'Should I beware of you too?' I didn't know if I was a bandit or not, I thought. I looked in her eyes and smiled, but didn't say anything.

'There's food and drink over there.' She gestured in the direction of another, more brightly-lit room, where we caught a glimpse of a big table covered with trays and bottles. Then someone called to her from the depths of a sofa. She called back that she was just coming. 'I'll catch up with you later,' she said, turning to Francesco, her eyes full of innuendo. 'Don't disappear on me like you usually do.' Francesco smiled at her, narrowing his eyes and nodding his head, with a nice, pleasant, spontaneous expression on his face.

As soon as he turned, this expression faded like a neon light at closing time. 'Let's eat something,' he said, like someone who's exhausted the conventions and now has to eat and then get down to work. I followed him.

The buffet was of a kind I wasn't used to. At the parties I went to, you'd get foccaccia, panzarotti, ham and salami sandwiches, beer and Coke. Here there was salmon, prawn salad, slices of bread with caviar, carpaccio of swordfish, and expensive wines.

We filled our plates, Francesco took an almost full bottle of white wine, and we went and sat down on a little sofa in the dimly-lit reception room.

'This is a good place to find candidates for our next game,' Francesco said, after cleaning his plate – we had eaten in silence – and emptying a few glasses. I nodded. Partly because I didn't know what to say, and partly because I was learning that it was often better to keep quiet than to speak. He took out a packet of cigarettes and lit one before he spoke again.

'I'm going to have a look around. You can wait for me here, or mingle, or have dessert. Whatever you like. I'll be back when I've finished.'

Again I said nothing, and he slipped away into the semi-darkness.

There were at least a hundred people here. Many of the men were in jackets and ties, others were more casual. My attention was drawn to one guy in particular: he was about one metre ninety tall, his head was completely shaved – not common in those days – he was wearing a tight black t-shirt, and he had big muscles like a bodybuilder.

He must have been about thirty-five or forty, and he was with a thin girl, about my age, who had the vaguely anorexic look of a model. She was beautiful, but there was something nervous and overexcited about her that was disturbing. The two of them together made me feel uneasy, as if there was something not quite right about them. As if there was a sickness eating away at them, just beneath the surface.

There were a lot of beautiful women here. Apart from the bald guy's girlfriend, though, I found it hard to focus on any of them. It was like being in a big, shiny luxury department store, full of attractive and inviting things. So many things you can't decide, because choosing one thing means giving up on others. I had finished the bottle of white wine and was about to light a cigarette.

'Can I have one too?'

I looked to my left, and up, towards where the voice had come from.

'Of course,' I said, making as if to stand up. Out of politeness and because I couldn't see her face properly. She touched my shoulder, told me to stay where I was, and turned me around. I smelled her sweet perfume. She sat down on the sofa in the place left free by Francesco.

'Clara,' she said, holding out her hand in a feminine way, leaning forward slightly in relation to the line of the wrist.

'Giorgio,' I replied, unable to prevent my eyes lingering a moment longer than they ought to on her large breasts. I recovered, held out the packet, lit her cigarette and then lit mine.

She took a drag and blew the smoke into the air. 'You're a very polite young man.'

'Why do you say that?'

'I notice the way a man offers a cigarette. Basically there are those who first pull one out and then hold out the packet, and those who just hold out the packet. That's what you did. You didn't force me to smoke the one you had touched. That would have been like sticking your fingers in my mouth.' She said these last words after a brief pause, looking me straight in the eyes. I inhaled slowly, as if giving myself time to ponder the meaning of her words. In fact, I was searching for something to say, something appropriate. I could smell alcohol. It was obvious Clara had already drunk quite a bit tonight.

'And what do you do, Giorgio?'

'I'm supposed to be graduating in law this year.' As I said this, I felt like an awkward schoolboy saying that he has been a boy scout for ten years. Clara couldn't be less than thirty-two, thirty-three. She wasn't pretty but she wasn't ugly. She had a predatory look about her. Not particularly intelligent, but predatory. I was making an effort not to look at those breasts that filled her white blouse so insolently.

'I used to study law, too. But I dropped out. I don't think I was cut out to be a lawyer anyway. I don't know if you understand what I'm saying.'

I didn't understand anything, but I nodded knowingly. 'And what do you do now?' I asked.

'Now I bring lawsuits against my ex-husband, who's a tight-fisted bastard who won't pay me what he's supposed to. But he will, I'm sure of that. Are you on your own?'

'No, I came with a friend.'

'Why don't you go and fetch us a drink, Giorgio?'

I stood up and grabbed a bottle of prosecco. She wanted to drink a toast to the two of us, and as our glasses touched I felt as if I was in another dimension, unreal and dizzying. And I felt like laughing. Not because there was anything amusing about the situation. It was a reflex, the kind I used to feel when I was a child and I was distracted in class – a frequent occurrence – and the schoolmistress noticed and lost her temper. When that happened, I always felt like laughing. It was a stupid thing to do because, of course, it only made her angrier. But I couldn't restrain myself, or rather, I managed to avoid laughing but instead made the kind of grimace people always make when they're holding back laughter. The same as now.

'You're not the kind of man who talks too much. I like that. Men always feel they have to smother you in small talk before they declare their intentions. Which are that they'd like to fuck you.' She held out her glass to me and I refilled it. She drank half of it straight down, and said, 'Would you like to fuck me?'

The whole thing was absurd. The impulse to laugh was greater than ever and I had to make a real effort to restrain myself. I don't know if I ended up looking inscrutable or just plain stupid. Not that it mattered: she had too much alcohol inside her to notice the difference.

'Yes,' I replied, when I was sure I was in control. I also had more than enough alcohol inside me.

She kept looking at me in silence, as if weighing up my answer, trying to grasp its hidden meaning.

At that moment, Francesco came back.

'Done,' he said, touching me on the shoulder. He smiled at Clara then turned back to me. 'Can I talk to you for a couple of seconds?' And turning to Clara, 'I'm taking him away for a moment, will you excuse us?' She looked at him without seeing him. Her eyes had become empty suddenly. Glassy.

I stood up and followed him towards the front door.

'Congratulations, colleague. I see you haven't wasted any time.'

'She made all the moves…'

'I know. Of course you can do whatever you like, but I want to warn you. She's unbalanced.'

'What do you mean?' I heard myself ask, resentfully. As if he had said that any woman who approached me at a party must obviously have something wrong with her.

'She has problems.' He touched his forehead with two fingers. 'She's a nymphomaniac, she drinks too much, and if you want my advice, if you're looking for a quick fuck I'd look somewhere else if I were you. Apart from anything else, with the number of men she's had, I wouldn't feel at all sure about having intimate relations with her. I don't know if you follow my drift.'

I followed his drift, and it made me feel ill. 'How do you know these things?'

'The fact that she drinks you can see for yourself. She's already drunk, you just have to look at her eyes. As for the other thing, apart from all the rumours, a friend of mine made the mistake of getting involved with her. They even had a kind of affair.'

'What happened?'

'The first night, immediately after they'd fucked, she made a scene. I mean, she went off the deep end, started screaming, told him he was a pig, just like all the others, he was only interested in fucking her, that kind of thing.'

Instinctively, I turned towards the sofa where Clara was sitting. She hadn't moved, and was still drinking.

'And what did your friend do?' I asked.

'Once he got over his astonishment he tried to calm her down. She did calm down, turned all lovey-dovey, and they fucked again. Then he left – they were at her place – and starting the very next day, she set about methodically tearing him apart. Sometimes she'd phone him and tell him she was madly in love with him, he was the love of her life, he was different from all the others, that kind of thing. Then she'd disappear and no one knew where she was for a week. That wouldn't have been a problem if the idiot hadn't fallen in love with her. So he went along with all of it. She'd tell him she was sleeping with other men and he was just a passing fancy. Then she'd cry and beg forgiveness and say – I remember this well – that he had to teach her how to love. And he stuck with her through it all.'

'How did it end?'

'It just ended. She got fed up with the game eventually. Assuming it was a game, because I think she's really out of her mind and has a kind of compulsion to behave like that. Anyway, it ended. More than a year ago, but he's still trying to pick up the pieces.'

Before he went on, he looked at me, as if to see if I had any questions.

'She goes to parties and clubs, looking for men, especially if they're younger than her. She takes them home – I suppose she's already told you she's separated – and the merry-go-round starts up again.'

We were silent for a few moments. Then I turned to the sofa again. This time Clara had vanished. I shrugged, as if to say, OK, end of conversation.

'So have you organised the next game?'

He had. We were playing on Saturday night at the home of someone with a lot of money, over in Altamura. So it was better if we didn't stay too late this evening. Fortunately, Giulia would still be ill, so I didn't think I'd have any problems. Francesco slapped me on the back and told me he'd introduce me to a woman who was worth it, another time. Then he walked away again.

'I'm going to spend a bit of time with Patrizia. Out of politeness, you know.' He gave me a knowing smile, and left me alone.

Suddenly I felt empty and uncomfortable. The excitement I'd felt a little earlier had turned into something else. Something unpleasant. So I wandered around, drank a few more glasses and smoked a few more cigarettes, just to kill time.

About an hour later, Francesco came back and said we could go.

9

THE NEXT DAY was a beautiful winter's day, cold and clear.

I was alone at home. My parents had gone out while I was still asleep.

My sister Alessandra had left three years earlier.

She still had a few exams to take to get her law degree when she informed the family that she had decided to abandon her studies. She didn't know where she was going with her life, but she did know – she said – where she *wasn't* going. She didn't want to become a lawyer, or a notary, or a judge. Nothing connected with any of the things she'd studied in the last few years. She hated those things. From the way she said this – and a few other things – it was clear she also hated our parents.

A few weeks later she left with a guy ten years older than her, whose ideas were as clear as hers, if you can imagine that. They went to London and stayed there for six months, working in a restaurant. Then they came back and went to live on a farm near Bologna. It was a kind of commune, well past its sell-by date. She became pregnant, and he went back to being free. He was convinced he was destined for great things and couldn't be tied down by anything as trivial as a family.

Alessandra had an abortion, stayed in the commune a while longer, and had other adventures with men, but I don't think any of them worked out. In the end, she came back to Bari, stayed with a girlfriend for a few months and then found a little apartment and a job.

She was a secretary for a works accountant, preparing pay slips for manual workers, clerks, waiters, and so on. Life sometimes plays tricks like that.

Every now and again, she'd pay us a visit and even stay for a meal. Whenever she did, you could feel the tension in the air. My parents would try and pretend that everything was normal, and sometimes Alessandra tried, too.

But everything wasn't normal. She couldn't forgive them for her own failure, their inadequate love, their clumsy concern. So, most times, the fiction couldn't be kept up and the resentment came to the surface. She would end up saying something nasty, even very nasty depending on the occasion and her mood, and then walk out.

When it came to me, things were no different from the way they'd always been, ever since we were children. As far as my sister was concerned, I simply didn't exist. I had never existed.

❖

After breakfast, I wandered around the house, switched on the TV, and went over my whole repertoire of excuses.

In the end, I sat down at my desk with the manual of civil procedure in front of me. But I had no desire to open it, and I had no desire to stay at home. So I went out.

It was unusually cold, even for January, but the air was clean and dry because of the wind, which had swept away all the dampness. Opening the street door, I felt the icy air on my face and ears. It wasn't a painful or unpleasant sensation. It was good to feel the cold. It reminded you that you had a face and ears and all the other parts of your body that weren't covered. My mood immediately improved.

I walked quickly towards the centre of town, spent some time looking in the shop windows, bought a shirt, and then went to the old Laterza bookshop.

Ever since I was a kid, I'd been coming in here whenever I was in the neighbourhood and at a loose end. I spent a lot of time in that bookshop. There were more books I wanted than I could afford, so I tried to read as much as I could while I browsed.

Sometimes I stayed until closing time and I always wondered if the assistants recognised me and had identified me as a persistent freeloader. I wondered if one day they'd ban me from the shop.

I breathed the good, familiar smell of new paper as I entered. It was Saturday morning and so there were quite a few customers, including several regulars. Many of them, like me, stayed a long time, read for free and didn't buy much. Among them, there was someone I'd always been curious about: a somewhat elderly lady – certainly over sixty – who wore a blue sailor-style jacket in winter, with a copy of *L'Unità* always sticking out of the pocket. She was a pleasant lady who always looked busy, as if reading books without buying them was a job of work for her. She bustled about from spot to spot, but was usually in the crime and horror sections, and very occasionally in the politics section. Sometimes she'd nod to me, and I'd nod back.

That morning, she was engrossed in what I assumed was a crime novel, as that was the section she was closest to. Our eyes didn't meet and I moved on.

I wandered past the history books, the sporting manuals, avoided the law books, and ended up at foreign fiction. There was a brand new book there, clearly a new arrival. It was called *The Foreign Student*. On the cover, against a light brown background, there was a kind of plaster statue of a young man walking with his hands in his pockets. The author was a French writer I'd never heard of.

I picked up a copy. If the book, as I suspected, had been put on display that very morning, I might well have been the first person to touch it.

I turned it over and read the blurb on the back page. Even now I remember parts of it by heart. It was all about youth and the 'fragile days when everything that happens happens for the first time and leaves an indelible mark on us, for better or worse.'

I opened the book, intending to read the first few pages, as I usually did.

I stopped at the page just before the prologue. There was a quotation by an English writer. I'd never heard of him either.

The past is a foreign country: they do things differently there.

I didn't turn the page. Instead I closed the book, went to the cash desk and bought it.

I went back home, impatient to read. In peace, lying on my bed, without being disturbed.

It was a beautiful, passionate novel, full of a heady nostalgia.

The story of a young Frenchman and his youth in America in the Fifties. A story of adventures, taboos violated, initiations, shame, love and lost innocence.

I read all afternoon, unable to put the book down until I'd read the last page. And while I was reading, and after I'd finished, and for a long time afterwards – even many years afterwards – I couldn't shake off the extraordinary feeling that, in some way, the story was about me.

❖

By the time I'd finished reading, it was time to go out. So I phoned Giulia, who was still ill, and told her I was going to the cinema. Who was I going with? My friend Donato and some of his gang: I made a mental note to tell Donato. Did I mind not seeing her another evening? Of course I minded, I missed her.

If she wanted, I said, bluffing, I could go round and keep her company instead of going to the cinema. She said no, as I expected. She said what she'd said the previous evening. There was no point in my making myself ill, and so on. All right, bye then, darling, see you tomorrow. Bye, darling.

I put the phone down and went to get changed. I was in a good mood.

I was free, and ready, and impatient.

10

THE GAME WAS at the home of someone our age, who lived in a residential area on the outskirts of town. There were five of us. Apart from Francesco and me, there was the host, the son of a builder, there was a guy who couldn't have been even thirty yet and was already completely bald, and there was an angular woman named Marcella, who had greasy skin and small eyes.

From the moment we were introduced, I felt hostile to all of them. They all looked ugly to me, and I thought they deserved what was coming to them. It's obvious I was trying to justify myself.

At least it's obvious to me now. At the time it was a quick, involuntary, effective way of stifling the last stirrings of my conscience. Whatever that word means. I needed to see them as nasty, ugly people, and so I *did* see them as nasty, ugly people.

The evening was similar to the first one, except that I knew how it worked now, and I liked it much more. As would always be the case whenever I played with Francesco, I felt as if this really was a game of chance. Only more intense. The certainty of winning didn't diminish the excitement: on the contrary it increased it. When we came to the decisive hands, the ones where we would make serious money, I felt a shudder at the back of my neck. When I was betting high and I threw down the cards and won, I forgot that what we were doing had nothing to do with luck. I was winning, and that was it.

By the time we left that evening, I had several hundred thousand lire in my pocket, in cash, and two cheques for six-zero figures. We'd won against the host and the angular woman, and I thought we'd done a good thing taking money off them.

I told myself I would have to open a bank account: I could hardly keep all that money in cash.

When I got back home, I went straight to bed and fell asleep almost immediately.

❖

We started playing regularly. Three or four times a month, five at the most. Usually in private houses and apartments, and very occasionally in illegal gaming clubs like the place we went after the bust-up at Alessandra's party. Francesco knew all of them, just as he knew a lot of places to go to at night.

Sometimes we even played more than once with the same people, but it was all part of a strategy. It helped to avert any possible suspicion. For example, after winning at the home of the fat man who owned the hardware store, we went back about ten days later and played with him and his surveyor friend again. They won – we let them win – a few hundred thousand lire and they had the impression they'd got a kind of revenge, and that everything was open and above board.

I was making five, six, even seven million a month, which was really a lot of money.

I'd opened that bank account. I could afford things now that I wouldn't have considered buying a few months earlier. Clothes, dinners in expensive restaurants, a ridiculously pricey watch. And all the books I wanted – that, more than anything else, made me feel rich.

And then I bought a car, a BMW – a used one, because I wasn't *that* rich. As I was about to sign the contract I had a moment of doubt, because I'd always associated that kind of car with a certain kind of person. But it was only a moment, and when I left the show-room at the wheel of that black, menacing, unnecessary object, I had a happy, mindless smile on my face.

Obviously I kept it hidden from my family, because it would have been really hard to explain away. I put it in a garage far from home, and to avoid suspicion, I would pretend to take my Mum's car some evenings.

'I'm taking the keys,' I would say ostentatiously as I went out. Anyone paying attention would have been brought up short. I was telling them I was taking the car, whereas before I would just take it and that was it.

They didn't even notice. But why should they?

With Giulia, things were going from bad to worse. We were head-ing for a break-up like a billiard ball rolling calmly and silently to-wards the hole after a small, decisive push.

There was a steady trickle of quarrels, a mixture of her incompre-hension and resentment and sadness and my lies and impatience.

I didn't have as much time to be with her as before, but that wasn't the point.

The fact was, I didn't *want* to be with her any more. Whenever we met, or went out, I was bored, distracted, annoyed by the banal-ity of the things she said and did. The only things I noticed were her defects.

After we broke up, she still tried to get in touch with me for a few weeks. It was pointless, and in the end she realised it.

I don't know if she really suffered because of me, or how much, or for how long. I've never spoken to her again, and on the rare oc-casions we meet in the street we greet each other coldly.

When we broke up the only thing I felt was a sense of relief, and I soon forgot even that. I had a lot of things to do.

And I was in a hurry to do them all.

PART TWO

LIEUTENANT CHITI WALKED into his office. Even though it was May, it was cold and rainy outside.

He had been in Bari for a few months now. Before coming, he had imagined it as a city where the summers were hot and the autumns and springs mild. What he hadn't counted on was winter in May.

Nor had he counted on being overwhelmed with work. Bari was considered a quiet place in the Eighties. A place where he could further his career, be promoted to captain, and so on.

It hadn't taken him long to realise that things were different.

Not only were there plenty of routine crimes – possession of drugs, bag snatching, burglaries – there were also major robberies, extortion, dynamite attacks, murders.

Something not unlike the Mafia lurked beneath the surface. Something opaque, like the stunted but monstrous creature you glimpse through the transparent shell of a reptile's egg.

And then there were all these sexual assaults. All similar, all clearly the work of the same man. Despite all the efforts they were making to find him, he was proving as elusive as a phantom. And it didn't help matters that both the carabinieri and the police were involved in the investigation, because as usual when that happened, they were all pulling in different directions.

There had been another assault last night. The fifth, as far as they knew. At any rate the fifth to be reported, because with this type of offence the victims often felt so ashamed, they couldn't even face going to the carabinieri or the police.

He slumped onto the chair behind his desk, lit a cigarette and started looking through the documents his subordinates had made ready for him.

The report from the patrol, brief details of the victim, statements by a couple of witnesses, if you could call them witnesses: two men who had seen the girl emerge from the entrance to a building, had gone to her aid, and had called 112. About the perpetrator himself, once again there was nothing. He really was a phantom.

No one had ever seen him, apart from the victims. Not that they'd really seen him either. He'd threatened to kill them if they tried to look at him, and they'd all obeyed.

Chiti was about to read the report that would be sent to the Prosecutor's Department when Corporal Lovascio appeared and said the same thing he said every morning.

'Coffee, lieutenant?'

Yes, he said, he'd like a coffee, and Lovascio went off to the canteen to get it.

The first few times he'd said, no, thanks, he'd go to the canteen and get it himself, there was no need for Lovascio to go to all that trouble. He'd meant what he said: he really didn't want to put anyone to any trouble, he felt uncomfortable having people wait on him. Then he had realised that Lovascio was hurt by these refusals. The corporal couldn't even conceive of an officer feeling uncomfortable because of something like that, and concluded that Chiti was refusing because he didn't like him. When Chiti realised this, he started saying yes.

He went back to the draft report. He knew he would find all kinds of linguistic errors in it. Some trivial, others quite unbelievable. He knew he would let almost all of them pass, and sign off on the report without querying too much. That was another way he'd changed. At first he'd corrected everything: syntax, grammar, spelling, even punctuation. Then he realised he couldn't go on like that.

The men were hurt, he'd spend hours on end trying to correct texts that were usually impossible to correct, and none of his superiors, in the Prosecutor's Department or anywhere else, ever noticed the difference. So, after a while, he adapted. He would still change a few things here and there, just to show them that he read everything, but, mostly, he adapted.

Anyway, he'd always been very good at adapting.

2

LOVASCIO CAME IN. As he had already brought the coffee, it had to be for another reason.

'Colonel Roberti wants to speak to you, lieutenant. He said he'd like to see you at once.'

Chiti put out his cigarette and closed the file. He was sure the colonel wanted to know if they had anything new on the assaults. The case was starting to get out of control and everyone was on edge. But there wasn't anything new, and the colonel wasn't going to like that at all.

The lieutenant walked along the corridors of the Fascist-era building that housed the barracks. He had no great desire to see the colonel, and wished his immediate superior, Captain Malaparte, hadn't been promoted to major and gone to take up a post at military school, leaving him alone, at twenty-six, to take charge of the team of detectives.

He knocked at the door, heard the colonel's thin voice telling him to come in, and walked into the room. He stood to attention, three metres from the desk, until Roberti, having assured himself that military protocol had been respected, signalled to him to approach and sit down.

'Well, Chiti, anything new on these assaults?' He'd been right.

'To tell the truth, colonel, we're trying to put together all the data we have in our possession. But of course we also need to look at what the Flying Squad have. Of the five assaults, three were reported to us and two to them. As you know, it's not easy to work with the police...'

'In other words we don't have anything new.'

Chiti rubbed his chin and cheek the wrong way, making his stubble rustle. He nodded, as if capitulating. 'No, colonel. We don't have anything new.'

'The fucking prosecutor is on my back, the fucking prefect is on my back. The fucking newspapers are on my back about this case. What should I tell the whole bunch of fuckers? What have we done up until now?'

Roberti liked to swear. He probably thought it made him sound virile. As he had a high-pitched voice, the effect was quite the opposite, but he would never know.

'The usual things, colonel. The first assault was reported at least three hours after it happened. The girl went home, told her parents everything and they came with her to the barracks. We sent a patrol over there, but obviously the place was deserted by then. The police are dealing with the second and third assaults, because in both cases the girls went straight to casualty, where the police have an officer on duty. We have managed to get hold of the police reports, though, and it seems like those assaults were pretty much the same as ours. They all took place in the entrance halls of municipal housing blocks, where the door is always open, even at night. We're dealing with the last two. In one case, the victim came straight to our barracks, on her own. In the other, the latest to date, two passers-by called 112 when they saw the girl on the ground, crying, close to the entrance where the assault took place...'

'All right, all right. But what actual steps are we taking? Are we tapping anyone's phone? Are we tailing anyone? Do we have any names? What do our informers say?'

Whose phone are we supposed to be tapping if we don't have any suspects? And what use are our informers? This guy is a sex maniac, not a pusher or a fence.

He didn't say that.

'To tell the truth, colonel, we don't have enough to go on to be able to ask the Prosecutor's Department for a phone tap. And obviously we've put pressure on all our informers, but no one knows anything. Which isn't surprising, as we're dealing with a maniac, not a common criminal.'

'Chiti, I don't think you understood what I said. We have to come up with answers on this case, we have to arrest someone. One way or another. I'm leaving Bari next year and I don't intend to do that with an unsolved case on my hands.'

He seemed to have finished. But then he went on after a brief pause, as if he'd just remembered something important.

'And this wouldn't exactly be the best start for your career here either, my dear Chiti. Remember that.'

My dear Chiti.

He tried to ignore the last remark. 'I've been thinking, colonel, perhaps we ought to consult an expert in criminal psychology. He could draw up a profile of the attacker. That's what they do in the FBI, I've been reading about it and…'

The colonel raised his voice, so that it was even more high-pitched – and distinctly unpleasant. 'What are you on about? Psychological profiles? The FBI? All that American crap, Chiti – that's not the way to catch criminals. To catch criminals, you need informers. Informers, phone taps, men on the ground. I want all the men on your team out on the streets, talking to their informers, putting pressure on them. I want plain-clothes patrols out all night. We have to get this maniac before the police do. Put together a few men with balls and get them working exclusively on this case, immediately. The FBI, the CIA, all that's for the movies. Is that clear?'

Perfectly clear. The colonel had never conducted a single investigation worthy of the name. Thanks to his connections, he'd spent his whole career in cushy office jobs, commanding battalions or teaching cadets.

The lesson in crime detection methods was over, and the colonel made a gesture with his hand to tell him that he could go. The kind of gesture you make to a troublesome servant.

The kind of gesture Chiti had seen his father make many times to subordinates, with the same stolid expression of arrogance and contempt on his face.

Chiti got to his feet, took three steps back, and clicked his heels.

Then he turned and left the room.

3

ANOTHER OF THOSE nights.

It always happened the same way. Chiti would fall asleep almost immediately, have a couple of hours of deep, leaden sleep, then be woken by a headache. A dull stab of pain between the temple and the eye, sometimes on the right, sometimes on the left. He would lie in bed for a few minutes as the pain increased, until he was completely awake. Every time, for those few minutes, he would hope against hope that the headache would pass as suddenly as it had come, and he could get back to sleep. But it never passed.

Tonight was no different. After five minutes he got up with his temple and eye throbbing. He went to prepare his forty drops of Novalgin, praying it would have an effect. Sometimes it worked, sometimes it didn't and the headache lasted a devastating three, four, even five hours. There would be tears in his eyes and a kind of muffled but implacable beating, nagging and rhythmical, inside his head, like the dull drumbeat of madness.

He swallowed the bitter drink with a shudder. Then he switched on the stereo, put on the first CD of the *Nocturnes*, made sure that the volume was turned down low, and went and sat down in the armchair, wrapped in his dressing gown. In the dark, because with a headache like that light was even more unbearable than noise.

He curled up in the old position as the music began. The same music his mother used to play, all those years ago. In other lodgings as cold and empty as these, while he listened, curled up just as he was now, and for those few minutes felt safe.

Rubinstein's piano had the texture of crystal. It evoked images of moonlit glades, familiar mysteries, dark, quiet places full of perfumes and promises and nostalgia.

Tonight the medicine worked.

He fell gently asleep, just when he needed it, surrounded by those limpid notes.

❖

Morning again. Time to go down to the office. The same building, the same claustrophobic journey through the service quarters, the canteen, the offices of the operations unit, the officers' mess. And vice versa.

Most of the furniture in his quarters had been supplied by the administration. There wasn't much that was his: the stereo, the discs, the books, and that was about it.

There was a full-length mirror on the wall near the door. A typically ugly barracks accessory.

It was hard to avoid looking at himself in the mirror every time he went out. Since he'd arrived in Bari, something had been happening to him more and more frequently, something that used to happen to him when he was about fifteen or sixteen, and which he had thought was buried in the remotest nooks and crannies of his teenage years at military school.

He would see himself in the mirror, examine his face, his clothes – trousers, jacket, shirt, tie – and he would have the impulse to break everything. Both the reflecting surface and the reflected image. There was a kind of cold rage in that impulse. A rage at that prosaic surface, that image of himself in the mirror, which didn't in any way reflect what he had inside him. Splinters, fragments, fumes, burning lava, shadows, fiery flashes. Sudden screams. Abysses he couldn't even look into.

That morning, he felt the same violent impulse.

He wanted to break the mirror.

To see his own image reflected in a thousand scattered fragments.

❖

That morning a so-called operations meeting was scheduled with the marshal and the two sergeants: the members of the team of detectives the colonel had ordered him to put together.

'Let's try and go over what we have, and see if we can come up with anything. We've all read through the files, so I'd like each man in turn to tell us what he thinks the five assaults have in common. You first, Martinelli.'

Martinelli was the marshal. He was a tough old character, who'd spent thirty years dealing with Sardinian brigands, Sicilian and Calabrian Mafiosi, Red Brigades members. Now he was in Bari, not far from his home village, for the last few years before his retirement. He was tall and bulky, with a shaved head, hands as big – and as hard – as ping pong rackets, a thin mouth, and eyes like slits.

No criminal had ever relished the idea of coming up against Martinelli.

He seemed uncomfortable, and shifted on his chair, making it squeak. He didn't like taking orders from an Academy graduate, Chiti thought.

'I don't know, lieutenant. All five assaults took place around San Girolamo, the Libertà area…no, wait, there's one – one of those the police are dealing with – which happened in Carrassi. I don't know if that's significant.'

Chiti had a sheet of paper in front of him. He noted down what Martinelli had said, and as he wrote, it seemed to him that this was all an attempt to make himself look good. He had an idea about how the investigation ought to be carried out, but it was all abstract. It was based on what he had read in books and, above all, seen in films. Maybe that bastard of a colonel was right. And these men, all of whom were more experienced than he was, probably knew it, too. It wasn't a pleasant thought, and he made an effort to dismiss it.

'What about you, Pellegrini?'

Sergeant Pellegrini was plump and short-sighted. He was a certified accountant: not exactly a man of action, but one of the few who could use a computer, and find his way through bureaucratic and financial documents. That was why they had taken him on to the team of detectives and kept him.

'I think we have to look through the records. We have to look for people with previous convictions for filth like this in the last few years and check them one by one, to see if they have alibis for the nights of the assaults. We need to find out if any of them came out of prison recently, maybe just before this whole thing started. At least, that way we'd have something to work on. I mean, these creeps never get out of the habit, prison doesn't take away the craving. If we find a lot of names that fit, I could start a database. As we go on we can add data and then cross check it... Well, anyway, you can find out a lot if you look in the records...'

At least this was a suggestion that might lead somewhere. Chiti felt a little better.

'What about you, Cardinale? Any ideas?'

Cardinale had become a sergeant early. One of the very few cases in the carabinieri where someone had been promoted as a recognition of unusual merit. He was short and thin, with a boyish face. Two years earlier, while off duty, he had been in a bank when a gang of robbers had come in. There were three of them, one with a pump action rifle, the other two with pistols. Cardinale had killed one and arrested the two others. It was like something out of a film, except that it really happened, and one man did die. A nineteen-year-old doing his first robbery. Cardinale was not much older at the time, and they had promoted him to sergeant immediately, and given him a gold medal they usually only gave to dead carabinieri.

He was an unusual character. He was studying science at university, which was why his colleagues regarded him with a mixture of diffidence and respect. He didn't say much, and could appear quite brusque sometimes. He had lively but inscrutable dark eyes.

'I don't know, lieutenant.' He paused, as if about to add something. As if that *I don't know* were only the introduction to some clear idea he had in his mind. But then he didn't add anything.

The meeting lasted another few minutes. They decided to do what Pellegrini had suggested and check men with records for sexual violence. To pull out their files, check when they'd been in prison, look at the MOs, take their mug shots – if there were recent ones, or make new ones if there weren't – and start to show them around in the vicinity of the places where the assaults had occurred.

Hoping to get somewhere.

Before the attacker did.

4

GIULIA AND I broke up at the beginning of April. A couple of weeks earlier I'd slept with another girl.

Francesco had introduced us one Saturday morning. Francesco and I were seeing each other almost every day now, even when we weren't playing poker. We were *friends*. It was the word he himself used, putting a strange emphasis on it. *Friends*. He said he'd had very few friends before me, maybe only two. Whenever I asked him about them, though, he became evasive. In fact he would become evasive every time the conversation touched on his private life.

Francesco, as I'd realised from the start, not only knew a lot of people, he knew many different kinds of people, and I really couldn't figure out how he'd come to meet some of them.

The so-called decent Bari of professional people, well-to-do families, beautiful girls. The world of shopkeepers and people with social pretensions, where he went hunting for prospective victims. The kind of characters who hung around underground venues. And the criminal element that haunted the gaming clubs and were involved in all sorts of shady dealings.

He had an extraordinary capacity for blending in. His behaviour, the way he talked, even the way he moved, changed according to the company he was in. And whatever the company he was in, he was always at his ease, or so it seemed.

That Saturday morning, we'd arranged to meet for an aperitif. By the time I arrived he was already in the bar, sitting at a small table with two girls I'd never seen before. They were both over the top: too carefully made up, too perfumed, too fashionably dressed. Too much of everything.

'Mara and Antonella, meet my friend Giorgio,' Francesco said, and smiled – a smile I knew well by now. The kind of smile he had when he was enjoying himself at other people's expense.

I shook hands with Mara and Antonella and sat down, and we ordered our aperitifs.

Mara worked in the offices of an insurance company. Antonella was studying to be a dental technician. They were both just over twenty, had horrendous local accents, smoked Kim cigarettes and chewed chlorophyll gum.

We talked about all kinds of interesting things. Like horoscopes. Or whether it was better to go to the disco on Friday or Saturday. Or the fact that they had recently left their respective boyfriends – both bores – and now they wanted to enjoy themselves. Mara was particularly insistent on this last point, but both of them looked us right in the eyes, to see if they'd made themselves sufficiently clear.

It was a beautiful day, and after a while Francesco suggested we all go and have lunch in a restaurant by the sea. The two girls raised no objection and we left the bar.

As we walked to the car, Francesco and I a few metres ahead of the girls, Francesco said in a low voice, 'We're going to fuck these two this afternoon.'

'What are you talking about?' I asked, keeping my voice down too.

'We'll get them a little drunk and then we'll fuck them,' he continued as if I hadn't opened my mouth. 'Not that we really need to get them drunk. They're already gasping for it.'

He was right, and I felt like laughing. Not that there was anything funny about the situation, I was just nervous. I made an effort to hold back the laughter, but it came out as a stupid smile, almost a grimace.

I could feel it on my lips. So I said the first thing that came into my head, to wipe away that grimace. 'Where are we going anyway?'

'Don't worry, I have a place. Let's take your car, it'll impress these two.'

So we took my black BMW, which did indeed impress the two girls. We went to a restaurant by the sea, outside the city, and had a great meal of raw seafood and grilled lobster. We drank chilled white wine and as the bottles and glasses emptied, the conversation grew thick with increasingly explicit – and increasingly crude – sexual allusions.

That was the day I discovered Francesco had a kind of pied-à-terre. It was a small apartment, two rooms plus kitchen. The furniture was new, and the place looked as anonymous as a hotel room.

It was four o'clock by the time we got there. Mara and Antonella were both pretty drunk. There were no formalities, no preliminaries, no discussion about how to pair up. Antonella and I ended up in the bedroom, while Francesco and Mara stayed in the living room, where there was a big black sofa.

My eyes and Francesco's met as I went into the bedroom. He winked at me.

It was like an obscene gesture, that wink, but I didn't realise it at the time. Or didn't want to realise it. So, once again, I responded with a smile.

A few moments later Antonella and I were throwing ourselves onto the bed, clinging together. What I remember most is her breath, which smelled of wine and cold cigarette smoke. While we were having sex – we did it several times, and at length – she called me darling, and I said to myself, Darling? Do I know you? Who are you? And again I felt like laughing like an idiot. Here I was, I thought, fucking this girl – a beautiful girl – and I didn't even know her. At times, I almost had to stop and make an effort to remember her name.

I should have felt uncomfortable, and yet all I felt was a kind of mindless elation.

During a pause, we lit a cigarette and smoked it together. She giggled and nudged me with her elbow at the noises coming from the other room. She even started to say something about it but then stopped abruptly. For a moment, she was completely still, with a strange, rapt expression on her face.

Then she farted.

It was a thin, prolonged sound, like a toy trumpet, in the semi-darkness of that strange room.

She put her hand over her mouth for a moment, then said, 'Oh my God, I'm sorry. It sometimes happens after I've had a good fuck. I can't hold back. It must be because I'm so relaxed.'

I was so surprised, I didn't know what to say.

What can you say in reply to something like that?

Don't worry, I also like to let out a nice noisy fart when I'm relaxed? Depending on my mood and what I've eaten, I also burp a bit? That kind of thing, just to put her at her ease?

I didn't say anything, and in any case she was already perfectly at ease, without any help from me.

She took my hand and moved it over her belly and then down between her legs. I let her.

It was evening by the time we left, and I realised I hadn't thought about Giulia once the whole time.

5

I WAS SUPPOSED to be taking civil procedure at the beginning of May – I was considered good enough to take it early – but I'd hardly opened a book in the previous few weeks. On the day of the exam, I went to the university like a sleepwalker, filled out the form and waited my turn. When they called the name of the person who was before me on the alphabetical list, I stood up and left.

It had never happened before. I had consistently high grades, and had never missed an exam.

Until that morning in May.

I left the university, feeling slightly dazed. I wandered around for a while, barely aware of what I'd done, but with a vague sense of imminent disaster.

Then I thought, what the hell, these things happened. I'd done the right thing not taking the exam, because I'd been a bit distracted in the past few weeks and hadn't studied much. I'd avoided an unnecessary bad mark, which would have affected my average.

No, I'd take one or two days off and then I'd get back to studying. I'd take civil procedure in June, or July at the latest. I'd graduate in December instead of in the summer. I'd still be ahead of all my friends who were doing the same course, anyway. There was nothing wrong with slowing down a bit. I'd been going too damn fast, up until now. What was the big deal?

Thinking these things calmed me down and I started to feel better as I walked home. I was pleased I never told my parents before-hand when I had an exam. I wouldn't be forced to make up any lies today.

I took those two days off.

Then I took some more, because I didn't feel ready yet to start again. And then even more, because I'd gone out too many times and been up too late at night, and had to catch up with my sleep during the day.

Then I just stopped thinking about it.

Apart from anything else, I'd been studying a new subject in the past few weeks.

6

ONE EVENING, WHILE we sat in the car, smoking and chatting about this and that, I asked Francesco why he didn't teach me some of his tricks. I said it like that, off the top of my head, one of the many things you say that never leads to anything. Of course, I liked the idea of doing what he did with cards, but I didn't think he would take my question seriously.

In fact, he took it very seriously.

'Are you sure you want to learn?' he said, catching me off guard. He always did things differently from the way you expected. I'd say something serious and he'd treat it as a joke. And I'd feel embarrassed, and start to think, maybe yes, when you came down to it, it wasn't really serious.

Or else you'd say something as a laugh, a joke, whatever. He wouldn't laugh and would look at you in surprise, almost offended, and not say a word. Or else he'd tell you that *this* was a serious subject, no laughing matter at all. And again you'd feel embarrassed or uncomfortable, and would think he was probably right and that once again something had eluded you.

He had this ability to pass judgement on everything in a way that seemed irreversible, and always with a hint of contempt for anyone who didn't agree with him.

All this I've realised since. At the time I simply thought he knew more about the ways of the world than I did, and had a clearer idea of how to behave in different situations.

'Manipulating cards, like manipulating objects, is more than just a matter of simple dexterity. The real skill of a magician is the ability to influence minds. Performing a magic trick successfully means *creating* a reality. An alternative reality where you're the one who makes the rules. Do you follow me?'

'I think so. As far as I can see—'

He interrupted me. It was obvious he wasn't interested in my reply. 'Anyone who tells you that life isn't a constant series of manipulations is either a liar or a fool. The real difference isn't between manipulating and not manipulating. The difference is between manipulating consciously and manipulating unconsciously. Take a guy who's only recently got married. One evening he comes home and tells his wife he's been invited to a reunion of old friends, or maybe a poker game, if we want to keep to the subject. Does she mind if he goes out? No, he can go if he wants to, she says after a short hesitation, but her face says the opposite of what she's just said in words. If you don't want me to, I'll stay at home, he replies. No, no, you go, she says, in words. Her face, though, says, It's obvious you don't care about me if you want to go out on your own. So then he feels confused, because he's getting these mixed messages, and he starts to get a bit rattled. It doesn't really matter, he insists, he can stay at home. No, she insists, in words, he can go. In the end, he feels so guilty, he *decides* not to go out. He can't accuse her of forcing him to stay, because she told him he could go if he wanted to. And he can't complain because he was the one who decided not to go out. So now he feels really uncomfortable. She's manipulated him, but neither of them know it, at a conscious level.'

I was looking at him: where was he going with this?

'Magic tricks – or cheating at cards – are a metaphor for everyday life, for relationships between people. There are people who say things and at the same time do things, and what they're really doing is hidden behind their words and above all their gestures. And it's different from the way it appears. Only the person doing it is aware of it and controls the process. The substance of things, their *truth*, is almost always different from what we generally think it is. Things really happen at times and in places which are different from those we believe or experience through our senses. Our true intentions are different from our stated intentions. Look, for example, at what really motivates people to perform so-called charitable acts. You won't like what you find. The truth is hard to bear, and not everyone can face it.'

I tried to get a word in edgeways, but it was impossible. He had to express his ideas fully, and he was just coming to the part that meant most to him.

'Look at poker, for example. Anyone sitting down to a game of poker does it because he wants to hurt someone else. You have to be cruel, it goes with the territory. Let's take a mediocre player who sits down to play, hoping his luck will be good to him and bad to his opponents. Now imagine that someone – an angel or a devil – appears to this hypothetical mediocre player before a game, and tells him he has a way of making him win a lot of money in that game. In return, he wants half of the winnings. Our player asks, how is this possible, and the other person tells him not to worry. He just has to decide: yes or no. If it's yes, he'll have to promise to give him half the winnings of that game. And that's it.

'What do you think our hypothetical player will do? Do you think he'll refuse because knowing in advance that he's going to win is a violation of the ethics of poker? Do you think anyone would ever refuse a proposal like that?'

I took out my cigarettes and lit one. Francesco took it from my mouth after the first drag and kept it for himself. As I lit another, he started speaking again.

'Our player will accept. He'll get a kick out of sitting down to play with the awareness that destiny is already on his side, and he'll enjoy every moment of the game. The only thing that'll bother him a little is that he'll have to share his money at the end of the game.

'Or else take a game between Sunday players and a professional gambler. I don't mean a card shark. I mean a professional poker player. What chance do you think these amateurs have against a professional? Do you think they'd have more chance than they would if they played us? No. They'd have exactly the same chance – none at all. The methods are different but the results are the same. Luck has nothing to do with it.'

His eyes glowed in the semi-darkness of the car. His cigarette had burned down almost to his fingers. The windows were down, the air was mild, and the silence was broken only occasionally by a passing moped with a souped-up exhaust.

'Until we became partners, you used to play poker normally. Do you remember the emotion you used to feel when you had a good hand and the pot was a big one? Was it any different from the emotion you feel now when you have a good hand, even though you know it has nothing to do with so-called luck?'

He was right. Damned right.

'People manipulate and are manipulated, cheat and are cheated constantly, without realising it. They hurt other people and are hurt themselves without realising it. They *refuse* to realise it because they wouldn't be able to bear it. A magic trick is an honest thing because we know in advance that the reality of it is different from the appearance. And in a way, on a universal level, cheating at cards is honest, too. I mean, we've taken control of the situation away from pure chance and put it in our own hands. I know you understand. That's why I chose you. I wouldn't say these things to anyone else. We're challenging the mindless cruelty of chance and defeating it. Do you understand? Do you? You and I are violating commonplace rules and choosing our own destiny.'

He'd said these last words in a curiously high-pitched voice. Now he suddenly broke off. He seemed exhausted. He took the packet of cigarettes from my pocket and lit another one, having only just put out the previous one. We were both smoking too much, I thought: I had a stale taste in my mouth. For a few moments, I felt dizzy. A sentence was going round and round in my head: 'It's all bullshit. It's all bullshit.' It was a weird phenomenon: I could see the words inside my head as if they were on a blank page, and at the same time I could hear them as if someone was saying them, also inside my head. I had a sense of them as an actual physical entity.

I didn't say anything, though, and when Francesco started speaking again, after rapidly inhaling half of his cigarette, those words dissolved.

'I'll teach you. You're the only person I can teach, because I know you understand what I'm doing.'

I nodded and then he asked me to take him home. He was very tired.

I started the car and switched on the tape deck. The BMW glided through the poorly-lit streets, as liquid as mercury.

Inside the car, the voice of the young Leonard Cohen was singing *Marianne* at low volume. Francesco was silent now, looking straight ahead. He was miles away.

Suddenly I felt alone and afraid and frozen to the bone. I remembered something from when I was a child, but it was only a vague memory and vanished before I could catch hold of it. Like a dream, the kind you have in the morning, between sleep and waking.

A sad dream.

7

TWO DAYS LATER, Francesco phoned me. I could come round at three o'clock in the afternoon, he said. To make a start.

I'd never been to his home before, had never even tried to imagine what it was like.

It was a dark, oppressive apartment, which smelled stale, shut in. The furniture was old. Not antique, just old and undistinguished.

The place was tidy, but in a strange way. There was something not quite right about it, just below the surface, something *really* not right.

I knew that Francesco lived alone with his mother, but I'd never realised until that afternoon how old she was. An elderly lady with a curt, hostile, resentful manner.

Francesco let me into his room and closed the door. It was quite a large room. The stale smell that lingered in the rest of the apartment was less noticeable here. A child's desk, covered with books. Books on shelves, books on the floor, even a few books on the bed. A large cardboard box full of Tex Willer and Spiderman comics. Walls bare except for an old poster of Jim Morrison, his face staring out into space. His fate already written in his eyes.

Francesco didn't say anything and wasn't even looking at me. He opened a drawer in the wardrobe, took out a pack of French cards, shifted a few books to make space on the desk, indicated a chair for me, and sat down on the other. Only then did he turn to me. He looked at me for a long time, with a strange expression on his face, as if he didn't know what to do. For the first time since I'd known him, he seemed vulnerable, and for a moment I felt a real affection and tenderness towards him.

At last he put the cards down on the desk.

'My father left home when I was thirteen. He was younger than my mother and went off with a woman who was younger than him. Much younger. A pretty commonplace thing, I suppose. Two years later he and his girlfriend both died in a road accident.'

He broke off almost abruptly, went to the window and opened it. Then he took an ashtray from a drawer, sat down and lit a cigarette.

'I never forgave him. I mean: not only for leaving us. I never forgave him for dying before I had a chance to make him pay for going away and leaving me alone. When he died I had a strange feeling about it, a really nasty feeling. I felt terrible grief and at the same time real anger. He'd escaped me. Damn it, he'd escaped me. I didn't think it in so many words, but that was the feeling. I'd thought so many times of how, as an adult, I'd confront him with what he'd done to me and rub his face in it. I'd be grown up and successful, and he'd be old and maybe desperate to rebuild his relationship with the son he'd abandoned so many years earlier. Too easy now, I'd have said. Too easy now, after you left me alone when I needed you. Too easy to die that way, without paying what you owed.'

He rubbed his face with his hands, moving them up and down vigorously, as if he wanted to hurt himself.

'Damn it, I really loved the bastard. I felt so alone when he left. Damn it. I always felt alone, after that.'

As he'd started, so he stopped. Abruptly. He picked up the pack of cards, did a few very quick exercises with one hand, and then said we could begin.

Now he looked and sounded like the Francesco I knew.

He took the queen of hearts from the pack, along with the two black tens: clubs and spades. 'Do you know the three card trick?'

I knew it in the sense that I'd heard of it, but I'd never seen it done in real life.

'All right, follow me. The queen wins, the ten loses. The queen wins and the ten loses.'

Delicately, he put the three cards down on the table, one next to the other. I could see clearly that the queen was the one on the left.

'Which one's the queen?'

I touched the card on the left with my index finger. He told me to turn it over. It was the ten of clubs.

How had he done it? He had put the cards down so slowly, I didn't see how I could possibly have got it wrong.

'Do it again,' I said.

He picked up the queen and one of the tens with his right hand, holding them between his thumb and index finger and between his thumb and middle finger. He picked up the other ten with his left hand, holding it between his thumb and his middle finger.

'The queen wins, the ten loses. OK?'

I didn't reply. I was watching his hands to make sure I caught every move. Again he put the cards down slowly, and asked me which one was the queen. Again I pointed to the card on the left. He told me to turn it over and again it was a ten.

He repeated the trick six or seven times and I didn't pick out the queen once. Not even when I just guessed, to escape the illusion of those hands moving so hypnotically and elusively.

It's hard to explain, to anyone who hasn't experienced it, the sense of frustration produced by such an apparently simple trick. There are only three cards. The queen is definitely there, and it's all happening right in front of your eyes, at a distance of a few centimetres. And yet there's no way you can find the queen.

'The odds for the person betting are very close to zero. Learning this trick is a good way to start. All the basic principles can be grasped immediately.'

He explained how the trick worked, and then he repeated it two or three times, even more slowly. To demonstrate the technique. Even now, now that I knew the trick and *knew* where the queen was, I still pointed to the wrong card.

Then he gave me the three cards and told me to try.

I tried. I tried again and again and again, and he corrected me, explaining how I had to hold the cards, how I had to let go of them, how I had to direct the other person's eyes away from the queen, and so on.

He was a good teacher, and I was a good pupil.

By the time we stopped, maybe three hours after we'd come into the room, my hands hurt, but I was already able to perform the trick to an acceptable standard.

I felt quite exhilarated, and was dying to show it to someone – maybe my parents when I got home.

Francesco read my mind. 'I shouldn't have to say this, but you should never show a trick to anyone until you've completely mastered it. Doing a trick and getting found out is frustrating but commonplace. Doing a trick at the card table and getting found out can be a lot riskier.'

I made a smug gesture with my hand, as if to say that he was telling me something obvious.

No, he didn't have to say it.

8

HE HAD BEEN having these dreams since he was a child. They were set in a vague past that may never have existed. In strange but comfortable places, filled with friendly presences. Warmth, anticipation, order, wishes, excitement, cozy and brightly-lit rooms, children playing, familiar voices in the distance, serenity, smells of food and cleanliness.

A sense of nostalgia, melancholy but sweet.

They were recurring dreams. There was nothing in them that had actually happened, no recognisable people, no places he knew. And yet – and this was the strange thing – he felt at home in these dreams.

Whenever he had them, it was always a terrible wrench waking up from them.

Very much like the time his mother died.

He wasn't yet nine. One morning, he had woken up and found the house full of people. His mother wasn't there. The wife of one of his father's – the general's – officers had come for him and taken him to her house.

'Where's Mummy?'

The woman had not replied immediately. First, she had looked at him for a long time with a mixture of embarrassment and sorrow. She was a big woman, good-natured and awkward.

'Your mother isn't well, sweetheart. She's in hospital.'

'Why? What's happened?' And as he said the words he felt the tears erupting, together with a sense of despair he'd never known until that moment.

'She's had an accident. She's … not well at all.' Then, not knowing what else to say, she hugged him. She felt soft and smelled just like their maid. A smell little Giorgio would never forget.

His mother had not had an accident.

The previous evening his father had gone out, as he often did. Official dinners, work, other things. His mother almost never went with him. She had put him to bed at the usual time – exactly half past nine – and had given him the usual kiss on the forehead.

Then she had gone to the remotest point in that vast apartment – the lodgings of the commanding general, the biggest of all – and locked herself in the servants' bathroom with a pillow and a small .22 calibre pistol which his father had given her as a present the year before.

No one had heard the gunshot. It was muffled by the pillow and dispersed through the dark corridors of that gloomy, overlarge apartment.

She had celebrated her thirtieth birthday that evening.

She would be thirty forever.

❖

Lieutenant Giorgio Chiti often thought he would go mad, too. Just like his mother. She had suffered from nerves, his father had told him many years later, in that icy, distant tone of his, a tone devoid of compassion or regret, devoid of anything.

Suffering from nerves meant mad.

And he was a lot like his mother. The same features, the same complexion. There was something slightly feminine in his face, just as there was something slightly masculine in hers as it appeared on those few blurred photographs and in his ever more faded memories.

He was afraid of going mad.

There were even moments when he was *sure* he would go mad. Just like his mother. He would lose control over his thoughts and actions, just as she had done. Sometimes this idea – madness as an inescapable destiny – became an obsession, an obsession he found hard to bear.

It was at such moments that he would start to draw.

Drawing and painting – along with playing the piano – were the things his mother had done to fill the long, empty days, in those lodgings tucked away behind the barracks. Lodgings that were always too clean, with the same shiny floors, the same smell of wax, all of them silent, with no voices to warm them.

Pitiless places.

Giorgio took after his mother in this, too. Ever since he was a little boy, he'd had the ability to copy really difficult drawings, and to invent animals that were fantastic and yet incredibly realistic. Half cat and half dove, for example, or half dog and half swallow, or half dragon and half man. What he liked most of all, though, was drawing faces. He loved doing portraits from memory. He would see a face, imprint it on his mind and later, sometimes hours or even days later, reconstruct it on paper. That more than anything else – that ability to draw people's faces from memory – had stayed with him as he grew up. They were always excellent likenesses, and yet subtly different, as if he had somehow grafted his own fears and anxieties onto other people's faces.

Faces. Mad faces. Unhappy faces. Frozen faces, distant and standoffish like his father's. Cruel faces.

Remote faces, full of melancholy and regret, staring into the distance.

9

THE RESULTS OF their trawl through the records had been disappointing. There were about thirty men whose records were compatible with the details of the assaults they were investigating. Some were rapists, some Peeping Toms, some had molested women in parks. They had checked them all, one by one.

Some were in prison at the time of the assaults, others had cast-iron alibis. Some were crippled or old, physically incapable of committing that kind of assault.

They had ended up with three men who didn't have alibis and whose appearance didn't clash with the shreds of physical description provided by the victims.

They had obtained warrants and had searched the men's homes. They had no real idea what they were looking for. Just something, anything, that they could link to the case. Even if it was just a newspaper cutting about the assaults. It didn't have to be a clue, just something to give the investigation the impetus it badly needed.

They had found nothing, apart from piles of porn magazines and other obscene material.

For a month, they had gone back again and again to the scenes of the assaults, looking for possible witnesses, anyone who had seen anything. Not necessarily the act itself, but a suspicious person hanging around earlier, for example, or someone who'd been past there again a little later, or on the following days.

Chiti had read that people like that sometimes liked to go back to the scene of the crime. It gave them a feeling of power, of being in control, to return to the place where they had committed their assault and go over what had happened in their mind. So he and his men had spent hours and days, showing photographs and talking to shopkeepers, caretakers, security guards, tenants, postmen, beggars.

Nothing.

They were searching for a phantom. A bloody phantom. There came a time – it was a bright, sunny morning in June, almost two months after the last assault, which made it the longest lull since this whole business had started – when Chiti thought they should wind down their inquiries for the moment. Although he didn't like admitting it to himself, Chiti hoped that everything would end like this, as it had begun. The same way he always hoped his night-time headaches would pass by themselves.

Two days later, the sixth assault took place.

Chiti had left his office and the barracks at dinner time. He told the sentry that he would be back about midnight, and in any case he could always be reached by pager. He had gone for a pizza, as usual, then walked around the city. Alone, as always, and aimlessly.

He had got back about midnight, a quarter of an hour after the 112 call had come in. A couple on their way home from the cinema had seen the girl coming out of an old municipal apartment block, crying. They had called the carabinieri and immediately two patrol cars had arrived on the scene. One had taken the victim to casualty, the other had brought the couple to the barracks to take their statements.

The girl was still in casualty when Chiti got back, but they'd almost finished with her and she'd be brought to the barracks very soon.

The couple – a husband and wife, both retired schoolteachers – hadn't been able to tell them anything remotely useful. They had been on their way home from the cinema when they had heard sobs coming from a doorway – they had passed it a few moments earlier, the wife said – had looked back and had seen the girl come out.

Had they noticed anyone immediately before that, or immediately after? No, they hadn't noticed anyone. Of course, there'd been cars passing, and they couldn't rule out the possibility that while they were attending to the girl, someone might have passed on foot. In fact, someone must have passed, the wife said – she was clearly the boss – but they couldn't say they had *noticed* him, or were able to provide any kind of description.

And that was it.

As they were signing their pointless statement, the girl arrived, accompanied by a man of about fifty who looked as if he didn't quite know what was going on. Her father.

She was short and round, neither pretty nor ugly. Nondescript, Chiti thought, as he asked her to sit down in front of the desk.

God knows the criteria he uses to choose them, he thought while Pellegrini positioned the paper for the statement in the new electronic typewriter – he was the only person who knew how it worked.

'How are you feeling, signorina?' Chiti asked, realising as he did so what a stupid question it was.

'A little better now.'

'Do you feel up to telling us what happened, what you remember?'

The girl lowered her head and said nothing. Chiti looked around for Marshal Martinelli and made a sign with his eyes in the direction of the girl's father, who was sitting on a small sofa. Martinelli understood. He asked the man if he wouldn't mind going with him into the next room. Just for a few minutes.

'I imagine you felt uncomfortable telling us what happened in front of your father.'

The girl nodded but still said nothing.

'And I realise you may also be embarrassed to talk to all these men. We could find a female psychologist or social worker and have her sit in, if that's any help.' As he said this, he wondered where the hell he was going to find a psychologist or social worker at this hour. But the girl said, no, thanks, there was no need. As long as her father wasn't there.

'So would you like to tell us what happened? Take your time, and start from the beginning.'

She had gone out with three girlfriends, as she often did. They didn't have any boys with them. They had gone to a club in the centre of town for a drink and a chat and at about eleven thirty she and one of the girls had left. They had classes at the university the following day and they didn't want to stay up late. They had walked part of the way together and then had said goodnight and gone their separate ways.

No, she'd never had any trouble going home at night on her own. No, she hadn't read anything in the newspapers or seen anything on TV about the other assaults.

When it came to the assault itself, Caterina – that was her name – was obviously vaguer. It was about five minutes, maybe less, since she'd said goodnight to her friend. She was walking at a normal pace. She hadn't noticed anything or anyone unusual. Suddenly, someone had hit her hard on the back of the head. It was like a punch, or a blow from a blunt instrument. When she'd come to, she was in the entrance hall of an old apartment block. He had made her kneel. There was a bad smell in the place, she remembered, a smell of rubbish, rotting food, cat's pee. And she remembered the man's voice. It was calm and metallic. He seemed perfectly in control of himself. He had told her to do things. He had told her to keep her eyes closed and her head down, and not even try to look him in the face. He had told her that if she disobeyed he would kill her with his bare hands, right there. But he said all this in the same calm voice, as if he was doing a job he was used to. And she had obeyed.

Once he'd finished, he had punched her again. Very hard, in the face. Then he had told her not to make any noise, not to move and to count to three hundred. Then, and only then, she could get up and go. He told her that he wanted to hear her start counting aloud. She had obeyed, and had counted to three hundred, aloud, in that dark, fetid, deserted entrance hall.

No, she couldn't describe him. She had the impression he was tall, but she couldn't be any more specific than that.

And she hadn't seen his face, not even in passing.

Would she at least be able to recognise his voice if she heard it again?

The voice, yes, the girl said. She would never, ever, forget it.

When the girl had finished her statement, Chiti made her sign it, and told her to call them if she remembered anything more about the man, or if she needed anything at all. She nodded at everything Chiti said to her. Mechanically, like a slightly defective clockwork device.

When she left the room, she moved in the same way.

10

FROM THAT AFTERNOON on, studying card tricks became my main occupation. My *only* occupation.

I would wake up in the morning when my parents had already gone out. I would wash, dress, check that the law books I should have been studying – and which my parents thought I was still studying – were in full view on my desk, take out the cards, and practise for hours. In the afternoon I'd do the same, only then I had to be more careful because my mother was usually at home and I had no intention of talking to her about my academic commitments.

A couple of times a week, I went to Francesco's place for my lesson. He told me I had a lot of talent: nimble hands and a willingness to learn. Within a short time, I was able to do things I'd never even dreamed of.

The three card trick in particular. I got so good, it sometimes occurred to me that I ought to go the gardens of the Piazza Umberto, sit down on a bench, and challenge some passing idiot to bet on where the queen of hearts was.

I knew how to pretend to shuffle the pack – leaving it exactly the same as it was before I started – in at least three different ways. Once a hypothetical opponent stepped forward, I could then put the pack back exactly as it had been previously. I could do it with one hand, well enough to deceive any spectator – or player – who wasn't paying attention.

I could take the bottom card from the pack and deal it as naturally as if it had been at the top, and I had learned to place six cards of my own choosing on the top, just by shuffling in a particular way. Francesco could go up to twenty cards, but for a beginner I was doing extremely well.

Obviously I wasn't yet in a position to cheat at the gaming table. I didn't yet have Francesco's absolute self-control, that hypnotic ability of his to walk a tightrope with his eyes closed, unafraid to fall.

He was almost the only person I went out with in the evenings now, though occasionally we'd have company, always chosen by him. I saw less and less of my old friends. I was bored with them. I couldn't talk to them about the few things that interested me. The poker games, the money I was pocketing and spending with grim determination, my progress in the art of doing card tricks.

In the meantime it was starting to get hot. Spring was nearly over, and summer, as they say, was knocking at the door. Many things were about to happen, in my life and in the outside world. One of them was meeting Maria.

It happened one night when we played in a villa by the sea, near Trani.

Francesco had been invited by the owner of the villa, an engineer who owned his own construction company and had a whole series of law suits pending against him. As usual, I couldn't figure out how Francesco had come to meet him, or how he had managed to get himself invited. The man was about fifty. He could have been my father. Though I don't suppose my father would have appreciated the comparison.

When we arrived, we realised that there was a party going on. A lot of tables had been laid on a lawn as large as a tennis court.

Inside, in a kind of reception room, a number of round green baize tables had been made ready for poker. There seemed to be quite a few people keen to play. But there were also a lot of people who were only there to drink, eat and listen to music. Or for other things, as I would realise by the end of the evening. The male guests were all noticeably older than us. On the other hand I saw a number of female guests our age, all accompanied by men who were getting on a bit – dirty old men, I thought.

Francesco, as usual, seemed perfectly at ease. While waiting for the gambling to start, he moved among the groups of chattering people, butting into the conversations as if these were people he saw every evening.

About eleven, the gamblers sat down to play. The initial stake was five million each – rules of the house. We'd never before started with such a huge amount.

That night, everything seemed to be on a large scale. With a stake like that to start with, it struck me that anything could happen.

I was already sitting when suddenly, without warning, I was overcome with panic. It seemed to me that I was in over my head: the game was too big for me, too mad, too uncontrollable. I felt the impulse to run away from the table, and from that house, and from all of it. While there was still time.

The voices of the people around me merged into an indistinct hum, and everything seemed to be moving in slow motion.

Francesco realised that something was happening to me. I don't know how he realised, but he did. He was sitting to my left, and he moved his hand under the table and put it on my leg, just above the knee. I didn't have time to jump at the contact. He was already digging his fingers, hard, into the soft, sensitive area on the inside of my thigh.

It hurt, and I had to force myself not to show any reaction. Just as I was about to put my hand under the table, he let go and looked at me with a smile. For a few moments I sat there, stunned, until I realised that the panic had passed.

We played, and I won a lot of money. The most we'd ever won.

It sometimes happens that for no particular reason – or for no reason you can figure out – you forget the details of an event. A psychoanalyst could probably explain that there's an unconscious motivation for this selective memory. I don't know. What I do know is that I can't remember how much I won that evening. It was certainly more than thirty million lire, but that's where my memories stop. I don't know if it was thirty-two or thirty-five or forty or whatever. I simply don't know.

In any case, it was the biggest win of the whole evening and word soon spread among those who were still at the party that there was serious money being won at our table. So a group of onlookers gathered, far enough away from the table not to crowd the players, but close enough to follow the game. As far as Francesco and I were concerned, the game was over. We'd already played for the biggest pots, and the winnings were already in my pocket.

But we had an audience, and Francesco was a magician. So he decided we'd give the audience a thrill, free of charge. It was out of the question for me to win again. I'd already had two full houses, a flush and a four and won millions, and if I'd been lucky again that would really have aroused suspicion. Francesco had lost a lot, for appearances' sake, so once in a while he could allow himself the luxury of dealing himself the best cards. For the last hand, our audience had the privilege of witnessing both a full house of aces (me) and four sevens (Francesco).

It was pure spectacle, a masterpiece of suspense, which the audience watched with bated breath. By the end, Francesco's eyes were shining. Not because of the win, which was fake, but because of the show. For once, he was playing the magician. He was enjoying himself like a child.

After a grand finale like that, I really didn't understand how I could possibly have had that panic attack. It seemed to me like something that had happened a long time ago, instead of earlier that evening. Or that hadn't happened at all.

We settled our accounts and got up from the table. The one who had lost the most was our host, but it didn't seem to bother him. He wasn't someone who needed to worry about money.

It was very late, but there were still people wandering around the house and the garden. Francesco had disappeared, as tended to happen in these situations.

I'd started to feel hungry and was wondering if there was any food left.

'Are you only lucky at cards?' The voice was deep, almost masculine, with a hint of affectation, as if she was making an effort to conceal her original accent. I turned.

Short chestnut hair. Tanned skin. Not pretty, but with large, unsettling grey-green eyes. Taller than me. Quite a bit taller than me. About thirty-five, I thought as I looked at her, trying to think of a reply. I was later to learn that she was forty.

'Do you mean you won all that money because you're good? There's only one way to win like that.' She paused. 'You cheated.'

I felt physically paralyzed. I really couldn't move a muscle, or say a word, or even get her face in focus.

She had found us out and was either going to expose us or blackmail us. That was the thought that shot across my mind like a flaming arrow. I felt the blood rush to my cheeks.

'Hey, I was joking.'

The tone was one of amusement, though I still couldn't tell if she really had been joking.

Then she said, 'Maria,' and held out her hand. I shook it. She had a strong grip. On her tanned wrist she was wearing a bracelet of white gold with a very large blue stone. I've never understood anything about jewellery – and at that moment I didn't understand much about anything at all – but it did occur to me that all our winnings of the evening wouldn't have been enough to buy that bracelet.

'Giorgio,' I replied, as my brain started to work again and Maria's face came back into focus.

'So, are you good, Giorgio? Do you like taking risks?'

'Yes, I do,' I replied, feeling a tremor of excitement. What was I supposed to say? Was it a question that allowed for different answers?

'So do I.'

'What kind of risks…do you like?'

'Not gambling. That's artificial.'

You're talking crap. You try losing twenty or thirty million, or winning it, and then we'll talk about artificial.

I didn't say that, I only thought it. What I actually said was that she was probably right, but that I was curious to know exactly what she meant. Meanwhile I was taking a closer look at her. She had a lot of little lines at the corners of her eyes, rather fewer at the corners of her mouth, a very animated face, high cheekbones, and a white, feral smile.

There was something about her that reminded me of Francesco. Something in the way she moved or talked, something in her rhythm. I don't know exactly what it was, but whatever it was came and went as we talked. Maybe it was the way she had of looking you straight in the eyes, and then immediately looking away. It was something that attracted and repelled simultaneously.

She didn't tell me what her idea of *non*-artificial risk was. She made a few rather vague remarks – the way Francesco did whenever I asked him to explain something he'd said or done – and then looked at me with an expression that seemed to say, 'Of course, we've understood each other, haven't we?'

Of course.

Still talking, we moved into the garden and got something to drink.

Maria looked like someone who spent a lot of time at the gym. She told me she was married and had a fifteen-year-old daughter.

I said I found that hard to believe, and she smiled because I'd said exactly what was expected of me.

Her husband was a luxury car dealer and had a number of showrooms throughout the region. He was often away on business. She looked me straight in the eyes as she said this. Her gaze was so direct, I was forced to look away and drink some of my wine.

We were sitting in the garden when Francesco joined us. He stopped in front of us, and for a moment there was a curious exchange of glances between him and Maria. So curious that it didn't even occur to me to introduce them.

Francesco turned to me. 'Here you are,' he said. 'I've been looking for you for a quarter of an hour. Shall we go? It's nearly four.'

'Two minutes and I'm coming,' I replied.

He said he'd wait for me by the car, nodded goodbye to Maria, and walked away.

I turned back to her, feeling embarrassed. I wanted to ask her if we could see each other again, but I didn't have time and didn't know what to do. I mean, I didn't know how to go about things with a married woman. But she wasn't uncomfortable and knew exactly how to go about things.

She took a notepad from one of the gaming tables, the kind used to tot up losses and wins. She wrote down a phone number, tore off the sheet, gave it to me and told me to call her. I could call any time between nine in the morning and one at night.

I left the house without saying goodbye to anyone, joined Francesco in the car park, and we left. I drove at a hundred and ninety kilometres an hour. He put the seat back and reclined with his eyes half closed, smiling that mocking smile of his from time to time. We didn't say a word the whole way home.

❖

As I was undressing to go to bed – it was already morning outside – I noticed the bruise that was forming on the inside of my left leg, where Francesco had grabbed me to cure me of my fear.

11

THE NEXT MORNING – a Sunday – I woke up late, of course. Through the half-open door of my bedroom came the smell of food and home.

I was hungry, and I thought I'd get up and go straight to the table. I'd always liked having lunch just after getting up: something that usually only happened on New Year's Day and a few other special occasions.

There was no rush, no stress. I didn't have to decide what to do as soon as I got up. Especially as it was a Sunday morning.

It was a nice feeling.

Then, while I was still in bed, I felt a strange unease creeping over me. A sense of guilt mixed with an awareness of imminent disaster.

I was going to be found out. I'd get up and go to the table, my parents would look at me and see my wickedness written clearly on my face and at last they'd understand.

I was filled with sadness and nostalgia. I'd have liked to feel that old pleasure I used to feel with my family, but now I realised it was lost forever.

I had this sudden, intense hope that my parents weren't at home. Because if they saw me this morning, they would find me out. I didn't know why, or why specifically this Sunday morning, but I was sure it would happen.

I got up, washed, dressed quickly and went into the dining room with that feeling just below the surface, like a tingling under the skin, a slight but annoying fever.

The table was already laid. The TV screen was filled with painful, unreal images.

It was the fourth of June 1989. The previous day, Li Peng's army had massacred the students in Tiananmen Square. More or less at the same time, it occurred to me, as I was winning millions cheating at poker and flirting with a predatory forty-year-old woman.

I can still remember that long news broadcast, almost all of it about what had happened in Beijing, and then the image dissolves and I see my father tormenting the last mouthful of roast beef with his fork.

He was moving it from one side of his plate to the other without picking it up. He would take a sip of his red wine and then resume moving that small piece of meat between what remained of his mashed potato. My mother's famous mashed potato, I thought incongruously.

I was waiting. My mother was waiting, too. I knew it even though I couldn't see her face. I felt her anguish as if it was a physical entity.

At last my father spoke. 'Are you having problems with your studies?'

'Why?' I tried to look and sound surprised. It was a lousy piece of acting.

'You haven't taken any exams since last year.'

My father spoke softly, separating his words. And when I looked at him, I saw lines on his face, signs of a pain I didn't want to see. I looked away.

'Do you want to tell us what's going on?' he continued.

It was painful for him to say these words. He'd never imagined he'd ever have to say anything like that to me. I'd never been any trouble, especially where my studies were concerned. It was my sister who'd caused them a lot of problems and that was more than enough. What was going on?

It struck me at that moment that they must have talked often and at length about what was happening to me. They must have wondered if it was a good idea to talk to me about it or if it would only make things worse.

I reacted the way all third-rate people do when they're caught doing something wrong. I reacted the way someone who knows he's wrong and doesn't have the courage to admit it reacts. By attacking.

It was a cowardly thing to do, because they were weaker than me and as helpless as only parents can be.

What did they want of me? I wasn't even twenty-three yet and had almost finished university. The only reason they were attacking me was because I'd slowed down a bit. Was it forbidden to go through a bit of a crisis, fuck it? Was it forbidden? I screamed.

I ended up saying some very nasty things and then got up from the table. They stayed where they were, unable to speak.

'I'm going out,' I said, and left.

I was angry with them because they were right. Angry with myself, too.

Angry and alone.

At nine-thirty the following morning, Monday, I phoned Maria.

12

SHE HADN'T SOUNDED at all surprised. She'd reacted as if she'd been expecting me to phone that very morning. She said she was busy today but we could see each other the following morning.

You can come over tomorrow morning, she'd said. To her house. Naturally, to be on the safe side, I had to phone first. All right. Tomorrow then. Tomorrow. Bye.

Bye.

I sat there for a long time with the receiver in my hand. Amazed by the total absence of hints and innuendo in that call. Wondering where I was going.

Well, to start with, I was going to her house, tomorrow.

After phoning, to be on the safe side.

She hadn't said, Come over, we'll have a chat, a drink. For appearances' sake, at least. All she'd said was, Come tomorrow morning.

I felt empty, and at the same time excited in a facile, mindless way.

The consequence of this strange mental chemistry was a kind of slow motion short circuit. I was thinking without really thinking. A slow series of images started unfolding in my head, uncontrollably. My mother. My father. Both looking older than they really were. I pushed the images away with difficulty, and my sister appeared, out of focus. I couldn't see her very well.

What I mean is: I couldn't remember my sister's face. But it made me sad and I pushed her image away too. That wasn't so hard, but in pushing her out I let Francesco in. He, too, was out of focus. Then a flash of something from the past. Memories of junior high school, the first day of vacation at the end of the fourth grade. Why that one in particular? Why was I remembering that? A boy in floods of tears at a party, when I was a child. Why was he crying? I felt sorry for him, but I couldn't do anything to help him. Two older children laughed at him and I didn't say anything. I simply felt really humiliated and turned away.

Then other images, even further back in time. So far back, I couldn't distinguish them one from another. And all of them slow.

Everything was very slow, almost unbearably slow.

Something was falling apart inside me, and finally I got to the point where I couldn't stand it.

I went into my room and put on a Dire Straits cassette. Mark Knopfler's guitar drove away the silence and all the things crowding into my head. I took out the cards and started to practise. The music finished and I carried on practising, as if nothing else mattered. I didn't stop until I heard my mother's key in the door, about two o'clock.

My hands hurt, but my brain was clear and calm now.

Like a frozen lake.

※

After eating I went to sleep. A good method of escape. The perfect natural anaesthetic. When I woke up it was nearly six and, as I couldn't bear staying at home after the argument with my parents the day before, I went straight out.

It wasn't warm for June, and after wandering a little aimlessly, I ended up in my usual bookshop.

None of the regulars were there. In fact, no one was there when I went in.

As I started moving around between the counters and the shelves, I realised that even books no longer interested me.

I'd gone into the bookshop the way people go to a particular café or greasy spoon. Out of habit, because I didn't know where else to go or who to go to. The only person I ever saw these days was Francesco. And he decided when we met.

I picked up a few books at random and leafed through them, but it was a purely physical gesture. A gesture of boredom and emptiness.

My interest was aroused for a moment in the Games and Hobbies section, coming across something called *The Big Book of Magic Tricks*. I'd never heard of the publisher, I'd never seen the book before, and I've never seen it since. I leafed through it until I got to the chapter on card tricks, but when I realised it only described a few simple tricks for family parties, I put it back on the shelf, disappointed.

I was about to glance at the *Complete Guide to Juggling* when I heard someone calling me loudly – too loudly – by my surname.

'Cipriani!'

I turned to my left and saw this chubby guy coming towards me – from the section containing manuals for public exams, I noticed – and as he approached, with a big smile all over his face, I recognised him.

Mastropasqua. A classmate of mine from junior high school.

Unequivocally, unanimously recognised as the stupidest person in the class. Not the bottom of the class, though, because he had the obstinacy of a mule, and by studying eight hours a day he'd always managed to get just enough points in all subjects.

The two of us had never been friends. In three years we'd exchanged maybe thirty words. Mostly while playing football in the street after leaving school on Saturday.

I hadn't seen him since we'd taken the written exams for third grade.

He came up to me and put his arms round me.

'Cipriani,' he said again, affectionately. As if to say, I've found you at last, my old friend.

After holding me for several seconds – I was afraid someone I knew might come into the bookshop and see us – Mastropasqua finally let go of me.

'I'm pleased to see you, Cipriani.'

I heard my voice answering him. 'Me too, Mastropasqua. How are you?'

'Oh, I'm fine. Still watching my back.'

Still watching my back. It was an expression we boys had used in junior high school. Mastropasqua hadn't updated his vocabulary much.

'How about you, are you still watching your back?'

All our slang phrases of those years came back to me. A slang I'd abandoned and immediately forgotten when I moved up to senior high school. Mastropasqua clearly hadn't. He must have cultivated it, the way some people cultivate dead languages, because of their wealth of meaning and power of evocation.

'Yes. Still watching my back.' It was my voice, but as if it was someone else's.

'Well, well, Cipriani. I'm so pleased to see you. What are you doing these days?'

I'm cheating at cards, I've stopped studying, I'm planning to fuck a forty-year-old woman, and I'm breaking my parents' hearts. That about sums it up.

'I've almost finished law. How about you?'

'Damn it! You've almost finished law! Well, it was obvious you were going to be a lawyer. Anyone could see that from the way you used to do in tests.'

I was about to tell him I didn't have the slightest desire to be a lawyer. But I stopped myself. It wasn't as if I had any clear idea what

I was going to do.

'I started studying to be a vet,' he went on. 'But it was too hard. So now I'm going in for public exams.'

He showed me the book he'd taken off the shelf. *Entrance Examinations for the Police Force.* That was the title.

'If I can work for the State, who gives a damn about university? I won't need to watch my back ever again.'

I nodded in agreement. It suddenly occurred to me that I couldn't remember his first name. Carlo? No, that was Abbinante. Another genius.

Nicola?

Damiano.

Damiano Mastropasqua.

Mastropasqua, Moretti, Nigro, Pellecchia...

'Do you still play football, Cipriani? Right back, wasn't it?'

I hadn't played for months. But it was true, I played right back. Mastropasqua might not have been a genius, but there was nothing wrong with his memory.

'Yes, I still play.'

'Me, too. Once a week, on Saturday afternoons, in the Japigia fields. That's how I keep in shape.'

In shape. I couldn't help looking down at his distended belly. I guessed his trouser size at about forty-four, and he couldn't have been much more than one metre seventy tall. He didn't notice.

'You know something, Cipriani?'

'What?'

'One of my happiest memories of junior high school is when Signora Ferrari made us write a story and you wrote that crazy one where all the teachers and our classmates turned into animals and monsters. She gave you a ten – the only time she ever gave anyone a ten – and then read out the composition in class. My God, how we laughed. Even Signora Ferrari laughed.'

I was flung back into the past, as if sucked into a vortex. All the way back to ten years previously.

The Giovanni Pascoli State junior high school. In the same building as the Orazio Flacco senior high school, known as the Flacco. All the classrooms had bars on the windows, after a student, walking along a cornice for a stupid bet, had looked down. I was still going to elementary school at the time, but a few boys who were older than me had told me about the scream. You could hear it all through the school. It had frozen the blood – and the youth – of hundreds of boys and girls.

It was cold in the Pascoli and the Flacco. Because the building faced the sea and from November to March the wind came in through the cracks in the window frames. I could almost feel that cold now, the whistling of the wind, the smell: a mixture of dust, wood, boys and old walls. And from among those memories the image of Signora Ferrari emerged.

Signora Ferrari was a really good teacher, justly famous. We all wanted to be in her class.

She was a fine-looking woman, with blue eyes, short white hair and prominent cheekbones. She looked like someone who wasn't afraid of anybody. She had a deep voice, a bit hoarse from smoking, and a slight Piedmontese accent. When I was in junior high school, she was between fifty and sixty.

She couldn't have been much more than twenty when, on 26 April 1945, she had entered Genoa with the partisan brigades from the mountains, carrying an English submachine gun.

I don't remember her ever losing her temper, in my three years of junior high school. She was the kind of teacher who doesn't need to lose her temper, or even to raise her voice.

Whenever a student did or said something he shouldn't have, she would look at him. She probably said something, too, but I only remember the look she gave and the way she moved her head. She would turn her head, slowly, keeping the rest of her body still, and look the unfortunate student in the eyes.

She didn't need to lose her temper.

The ten she gave my composition was unique: the highest mark Signora Ferrari ever gave was eight. Or very occasionally nine. It was also unique for a composition – a humorous composition at that – to be read out in class.

And Mastropasqua was right: even she couldn't help laughing when she came to some passages.

I don't remember what kind of animal I'd turned the maths and science teacher into. But it must have been funny because when Signora Ferrari came to it, she really burst out laughing. She laughed so much, she had to stop reading, put the paper down on her desk, and cover her face with her hands. My classmates were laughing, too. The whole class was laughing and so was I, though mostly to hide the satisfaction and pride on my face. I was eleven or twelve years old. When I grew up, I thought, I'd be a famous writer of humorous novels. I was happy.

The image faded. Mastropasqua was saying something I didn't understand. He must have changed the subject. I nodded vigorously, half closing my eyes and making an effort to smile.

'We must have a reunion. I'll call everyone after my exam.'

A reunion. Great idea. Let's have one now and then another one after twenty years and another one after thirty years. I nodded again, and again made an effort to smile, but I realised that the smile was turning into a grimace. Great to see you again, Cipriani. You and your books, eh?

Nice to see you, too. Bye, Cipriani – another hug – Bye, Mastropasqua.

He walked off to the cash desk with his manual on how to pass the entrance exam to become a police officer. I stayed where I was, pretending to look at a book on bridge, waiting for my classmate to leave the shop. When I turned round, he was gone, sucked back to where he had come from. Wherever that was.

Then I left, too, and walked along the sea front, and then further, as if I was escaping from something, all the way to the southern edge of the city, to where the pavement and the buildings end. I bought three big bottles of beer from a stand and went and sat down on the stone base of the last lamppost, facing the sea, not looking at anything in particular. And not thinking about anything in particular either.

I stayed there for a long time, drinking and smoking. The daylight faded slowly. Very slowly. The horizon dissolved just as slowly. The day seemed infinitely long, and I didn't know where to go. There were moments when I had the feeling I'd never be able to get up again, never be able to move. It was as if I was trapped in a spider's web.

It was already dark by the time I got down from that block of granite, and in my place I left the empty bottles standing in a line, facing the sea. Before turning and leaving I stood for a few moments, looking at the three reddish-purple silhouettes against a background of Prussian blue. They must mean something, I thought, those bottles standing there facing the sea, waiting for someone to knock them over.

But of course I didn't know what they meant. If they meant anything at all.

I had to walk nearly an hour to get back home, with long, effortful strides. I felt dazed with tiredness and beer. I walked with my head down, looking at nothing except the metre of pavement in front of me.

I went to bed and slept for a long time. A deep sleep, with dreams forever out of reach.

13

ON TUESDAY MORNING it rained, steadily and insistently. It wasn't June weather at all.

The noise of the rain had woken me early and I hadn't been able to stay in bed. I'd got up no later than eight. It was too early to phone and I had to find a way to pass the time. So I had a leisurely breakfast, cleaned my teeth and shaved. Then, seeing as it was still early, I thought I'd tidy my room before getting dressed.

I switched on the radio, found a station broadcasting Italian music without too many commercial breaks, and started.

I collected together old newspapers, notes I didn't need any more, odds and ends left at the back of my desk drawers, and two old slippers which had been under the bed for God knows how long, and put everything in two big rubbish bags. I arranged the books on the shelves, and rehung a poster – Magritte's *Empire of Lights* – which had been hanging crookedly for several months, held up by a single flimsy piece of adhesive tape. I even dusted the room with a damp cloth. I'd learned to do that when I was a child and my parents paid me to help out in the house.

Then I washed and dressed, went straight to the telephone and, without thinking any more about it, called Maria.

Again a conversation without innuendo. Like a business call. Did

I want to come right now? Yes, I did. If she could tell me how to get to her house. From her number I assumed she probably lived in the suburbs, over towards Carbonara. When she told me, I saw that I was right. She lived not far from the tennis club, a few kilometres before Carbonara. An area where rich people had their villas. As I'd thought.

When I left home, the rain was still falling steadily from a heavy grey sky. I got in the car, sure that I wouldn't get out of the centre of town in less than half an hour. It was one of those days when the traffic is impossible. Usually it would have bothered me. Today, even if I was stuck in a jam, I found it relaxing to spend a long time in the car, listening to music – the same station I'd tuned to at home – and not thinking of anything, not doing anything, just letting the time hang there, suspended.

So I drove slowly through the city, between double-parked cars, puddles out of the Third World, dazed-looking people with short-sleeved shirts and black umbrellas, traffic police in oilskins. I listened to the radio and followed the hypnotic movement of the wipers sweeping away the raindrops from the windscreen. After a while, I realised I was moving my head imperceptibly in time to the windscreen wipers, and when I reached the vicinity of the tennis club I wouldn't have been able to say how exactly I'd got there.

The garden of the villa was surrounded by a wall of ochre bricks, at least two metres high, with a hedge of cedars protruding above it, their leaves iridescent, somewhere between moss green and turquoise. The rest of the world was in black and white.

I got out by the gate, rang twice at the entryphone, and got back in the car without waiting for an answer. I had the feeling, at that moment, that I was moving as if I'd been programmed. Not a single gesture I was making had been determined by me.

The automatic gate opened suddenly, noiselessly, as if in a dream.

As I carefully drove forward and glimpsed a two-storey villa in the distance, I was overcome with anxiety. I had a strong sense of unreality and an urge to escape.

Everything was unreal and irremediably strange. The car advanced slowly along the drive between tall pines, and I thought of making a U-turn and driving away. But when I looked in the rearview mirror I saw the gate closing, as silently as it had opened.

The car kept moving. Of its own volition. Right up to the villa.

There was a kind of portico, and Maria was standing beneath it, pointing to the right. I didn't understand at first, I thought she was telling me to get out of there. Something unexpected had cropped up – maybe her husband had returned? – and I had to escape. For a few moments I felt a mixture of panic and relief.

Then I realised she was only pointing me towards a parking space. There was an ivy-covered canopy and I left the car beneath it, next to an old Lancia that seemed to have been there for a very long time. There was also a dark-coloured runabout. Maria's car, I assumed. As I walked from the parking space to the portico, with the rain falling on me, I had the impression I was moving in slow motion.

She said Hi, come in, and went inside the house while I was still replying to her greeting. Inside, everything was excessively tidy, and there was a smell of some scented detergent.

We went into the kitchen and had some fruit juice and talked for a while. The only thing I remember of what she said is that the maid would be there at lunch time because she didn't like having people in the house in the morning. I'd be gone by then.

We were still in the kitchen when she pressed her mouth to mine. She had a hard, dry, fleshy tongue. I could smell the perfume she'd put on her neck just before I got there. There was too much of it, and it was too sweet.

I don't remember exactly how we ended up in the bedroom. It obviously wasn't her and her husband's room. The guest room maybe. Or one specially set aside for clandestine fucks. It was clean and very tidy, with twin beds placed side by side, a clear wooden sideboard and a window looking out on the garden. I could see two palms out there, with a hedge behind them.

The house was silent, and from outside the only noise was the tap-tap of the rain. No sounds of cars, no sounds of people. Nothing. Only the rain.

Maria had a dry, muscular body. The result of hours and hours in the gym. Aerobics, body building, God knows what else.

But at one point, as I lay on my back and she moved above me, I saw the stretch marks on her breasts. The image of that moment – those aging breasts on an athletic body – has stayed in my memory with photographic precision.

A sad, indelible image.

As she moved methodically, joined to my body – and I moved, too, as if doing a gymnastics exercise – I felt my nostrils filling with that excessively sweet perfume and another, less artificial smell that was just as alien.

As we approached a climax, she called me Darling. Once. Twice. Three times.

Then many times. Faster and faster. It was like that children's game where you keep repeating a word until the brain goes into a kind of short circuit and you lose sight of the meaning.

Darling.

Afterwards, I wanted to light a cigarette but didn't. She hated cigarette smoke, she'd told me. So I didn't move, just lay on my back, naked, while she talked. She also lay on her back, naked. Every now and again she would pass a hand over her ribs, as if she was soaping herself.

She talked, and I held my breath, and the rain kept falling, and time seemed to stand still.

I have no memory of getting dressed, or retracing the steps that had brought us to that guest room, or arranging to meet again, or saying goodbye. Some images of that morning are still very clear in my mind, like a series of photos. Others vanished immediately.

When I left, it was still raining.

14

UP UNTIL THAT Tuesday in June my memories follow one another in normal chronological order. After it, things seem to speed up, in a surreal, syncopated rhythm. It's all a jumble of scenes, some in colour, some in black and white, some with a bizarre non-synchronised soundtrack.

I can only see these scenes from the outside, like a spectator.

Many times, over the years, I've made the effort to think myself back into the situations I lived through. I've tried to see the scenes again from the same positions I was in when they happened, but I've never managed it.

Even now, as I write, I keep trying, but as soon as I seem to be getting there, a kind of invisible elastic band makes me leap back and I lose my bearings. When I try to get the scene back into focus, I'm a spectator again. From a different angle, sometimes closer, sometimes from a distance. Sometimes – and this is a little scary – from above.

But always as a spectator.

❖

I saw Maria quite often after that. Almost always in the morning, but sometimes also late at night. The house was always silent and very clean. Whenever I left, I'd be feeling slightly nauseous, and to get over that feeling I'd tell myself that this was the last time.

A few days later I'd phone again.

I don't remember a single conversation with my parents. I was trying to avoid seeing them, and whenever I saw them I would avoid looking at them.

I would get home late at night, and stay in bed until late in the morning. I would go out, go to the sea or to Maria's house, or simply drive around with the air conditioning on and the music at full volume. I would get back late in the afternoon, wash, change, and go out again, and finally get home in the middle of the night.

I remember many poker games, both before and after our trip to Spain.

Games in air-conditioned rooms stagnant with smoke, games on terraces, games in the gardens of houses by the sea. Once even on a boat.

And once in a gaming club. That one I'll never forget.

Francesco didn't usually like playing in gaming clubs. He said it was dangerous and exposed us to needless risks. Those clubs are a closed environment, rather like the world of the drug addict. Everyone knows everyone else. At the pace we were going – four, five, even six games a month – they'd soon recognise us. They would notice that I almost always won. Then they would notice that we were always together. Finally someone would watch us, and would notice that I always won the most when Francesco was dealing.

So we generally played well away from those circles, thanks to Francesco's incredible capacity for always finding new places to play, often outside Bari, and new people to play against. Almost all of them were amateurs, and if we ever saw them again it would only be once, for a return match.

How Francesco managed to arrange so many games, with so many people who didn't know each other, I could never understand.

Over the months, there'd been a gradual change in the kind of people we played against. At first they were always people with money, lots of money. People for whom losing five, six, ten million lire at the poker table was a bother, but not a personal or family tragedy. Over time, I'd seen fewer and fewer of these people at our games. Over time, we'd started playing more and more often with clerks, a few students like us, a few manual workers, even a few pensioners. Sometimes not much more than down and outs. Sometimes less. They lost like rich people, but it wasn't quite the same for them.

This wasn't the way it was meant to be when we'd originally come to an understanding. It was if we were on a slippery slope.

Towards what, I didn't want to know.

⁂

A bald man in a vest, with tufts of black hair on his shoulders, was sitting at the front door of the club. I told him I had come to see Nicola. I had no idea who Nicola was, it was what Francesco had told me to say. The bald man looked around, moving only his eyes, and then jerked his head towards the interior. I crossed a large room. It was hot in there and the old, wheezy air conditioning didn't make it any cooler. The room was filled with dozens of innocent-looking video games. Star Wars games, car races, shoot-outs, that kind of thing. There weren't many people at the machines that evening. They were all adults and as I crossed the hall I wondered vaguely what games they were playing. Francesco had told me that many of these machines were equipped with a device – activated by remote control or even just a key – which transformed them into lethal poker games. The customer would ask the manager if he could play. If he was a stranger, he'd be told curtly that there were no video poker games in the club. Just in case he was a policeman or a carabiniere. If, on the other hand, the customer was already known or was introduced by someone, the manager would transform the machine by turning the key or pressing a button on the remote. There were people who spent hours and hours there, playing a few thousand lire at a time, and ended up losing millions. If the machine didn't receive an impulse in fifteen seconds, the innocent legal game would automatically reappear on the screen. Which was what the police saw if they came in to check the place out, maybe after receiving an anonymous letter from some desperate wife.

From the videogames room you went through into another room, a smaller one, with three billiard tables. No one was playing, the air conditioning was slightly more effective, and there was another guy who asked who I was looking for. I was still looking for Nicola.

The man told me to wait there. He went to a small metal door at the far end of the room and spoke into an entryphone, saying something I couldn't hear. Less than a minute later, Francesco appeared and signalled to me to come in. We walked along a corridor dimly lit by a naked bulb and down a steep, narrow staircase until at last we reached our destination. It was a low-ceilinged cellar with six or seven round green tables, all except one already occupied. At the far end, opposite the door, was a kind of bar. Behind it, a gaunt, mean-looking elderly man.

The air conditioning worked well here. A bit too well: I shivered with cold as I entered. The room had that stale smell you find in places where people smoke a lot and the only change of air is provided by the air conditioning. A green lampshade hung above each table, as if to lend a professional tone to this gambling den on the outskirts of town. The overall effect was something between the surreal and the squalid. A dimly lit cellar, cones of yellow light, wisps of smoke forming vaguely malign-looking spirals, men sitting astride their chairs between the lights and the surrounding dark.

We went to the bar and Francesco introduced the old man and two nondescript guys who were going to play with us. We were waiting for someone else: there'd be five of us playing tonight. While we waited, Francesco explained the house rules.

To get a table you paid half a million to the manager. So, as there were five of us, we'd have to pay a hundred thousand lire each. In return we'd get a new pack of cards, chips, and the first coffee. As well as the right to play all night. To get more coffee, alcoholic drinks, or cigarettes, you had to pay a supplement. The initial stake was five hundred thousand lire and at the end of the game you had to give the manager five per cent of your winnings. If you won, of course.

The fifth man arrived a few minutes later. He apologised profusely for the delay, breathing heavily and wiping the sweat from his face with an old-fashioned white handkerchief. Everything about him looked slightly incongruous. He was wearing a white shirt with the kind of collar that was about thirty years out of date. His grey hair was slightly too long, and the index finger and middle finger of his left hand were yellowed with nicotine.

His eyes, framed by deep, dark rings, were curiously gentle, with flashes of anxiety in them. He was clean-shaven and smelled of aftershave. It was a smell that reminded me of my early childhood. I must have smelled it on my grandfather, or my uncle, or someone else who was already very big when I was very small. Something out of the past.

He seemed like something out of the past, as if he had emerged from a neo-realist film or an old black and white newsreel.

He was a lawyer, or at least that was what he was introduced to me as. I don't remember his surname. Everyone called him Gino the lawyer or just Gino.

We sat down at the table, and they brought us coffee, cards and chips. I was about to take out my wallet to pay the fee, but Francesco stopped me with a glance and a slight nod. This wasn't a place where you paid in advance. The owners, whoever they were, didn't have any problems with customers being insolvent.

I don't know how many hours we played, but it was definitely longer than usual. When I look back at the scene now, I see a fog, composed of cigarette smoke, artificial light and shadows. Almost the only things that emerge from this fog are the face and gestures of Gino the lawyer, in a series of still photos, quite separate from each other. I don't remember the names or faces of the other players. If I'd passed them in the street the next day, I probably wouldn't have recognised them.

All through the game, I kept my eyes on that fifty-something lawyer, with his heavy breathing, his permanently lit cigarette – he smoked the strongest kind of MS's – and his apparently imperturbable expression. For some reason, he drew my attention. I was hypnotised by him.

Noting again that he was clean-shaven, it occurred to me that he must have shaved just before coming here. To this dirty, smoke-filled cellar, filled with crooks and delinquents of all kinds, including me.

He's the same age as my father, I thought after a while, and I felt uncomfortable.

Whenever he lost, the left corner of his mouth would tremble slightly. A moment later, though, he would smile, as if to say, 'No need to worry about me, *really*, there's no need to worry about me. What does it matter if I lose one pot?'

He lost a lot of pots. He bet on every game. He played in a way that was both methodical and febrile. As if he didn't care at all about the money that lay there on the table in the form of those dirty chips. Maybe it was true, in a way. Maybe he was sitting there for a reason other than money.

And yet there was something sick, feverish, about the very calm way he moved the chips into the pot, even though he rarely got them back at the end of the hand.

He would have lost even if we hadn't been there.

We stopped playing at four in the morning. The other tables were empty when we stood up, almost all the lights had been turned out, and an unsettling greyish cloud hung in the air.

Naturally I won, and one of the nondescript guys also won, though much less than me. Francesco would later tell me that he was someone you'd do best always to settle your accounts with. And make sure you didn't upset him. That was why he had let him win. He wanted everything to go as smoothly as usual, without snags of any kind.

The others, Francesco included, lost. Gino the lawyer most of all. He took his umpteenth cigarette out of the crumpled and now almost empty packet, lit it, and said that if I didn't mind he would pay by cheque, because obviously he didn't have all that much cash on him. If I didn't mind, he'd also postdate the cheque. There was nothing to worry about because he was expecting some money from a client. It would only be two or three days. But to be on the safe side, if I didn't mind, he would postdate the cheque by a week. I said that was fine by me, though for some reason I avoided looking at Francesco as I said it.

We paid the old man, Francesco paid – in cash – the nondescript man you'd do best always to settle accounts with, a few more banknotes were passed from hand to hand, and I ended up with a post-dated cheque. The handwriting was elegant and nervous. Aristocratic, I caught myself thinking. Such a contrast with the man's haggard appearance. As if it were the last vestige of the person he must once have been. Some time in the past, long ago.

15

A FEW DAYS later, on the date indicated on Gino the lawyer's cheque, we went to the bank to cash it and divide the money. As usual.

The cashier ran the usual checks and then said he was sorry but the account was overdrawn and they couldn't accept the cheque. This had never happened before and I felt, absurdly, as if I'd been caught in the act. I was sure the cashier was going to ask me how I had got hold of that cheque, as well as a whole lot of other questions, and, seeing the guilty look on my face, would find me out. The silence only lasted a few seconds, but they seemed very long. I didn't know what to say. I'd rather not have been there, however I'd got there.

Then I heard Francesco's voice, just behind me. He asked the cashier to give us back the cheque, because obviously there'd been a misunderstanding with the client. Those were his exact words: 'There must have been a misunderstanding with the client.' These things happened. There was no need to make it official, no need to re-present the cheque, we'd handle it ourselves. Thank you and have a nice day.

A few moments later we were outside the bank, in the sultriness of the Bari summer.

'The asshole. I should have expected this.' For the first time since I'd got to know him, Francesco seemed angry. Really angry. 'It's my fault. We shouldn't play in gaming clubs and we shouldn't play with people like that. Damn it.'

'What do you mean, people like that?'

'Gambling addicts. Compulsive players. That's what he was.'

There was rage and contempt in what Francesco was saying and the way he was saying it. For some reason I found this quite natural, even though I didn't understand why.

'Did you see how he played?'

He paused, but it wasn't to hear my answer. In fact, I didn't say anything.

'People like him play the way other people take heroin. They're junkies. And you can't trust them, any more than you can trust junkies. They'd rob their own mothers, fathers, wives, their own children to be able to play one more time. They borrow money from their friends and never pay it back. They think they know how to play, and to hear them talk they always have some foolproof scientific system that means they can't fail. But then when they sit down to play, they play like madmen. And when they lose they immediately want to play again. They always want more. They need it, because playing makes them feel alive. Cheapskates, all of them. There's nobody I'd trust less than one of those people. And yet I sat down to play with one of them, knowing what he was. It's my fault.'

Francesco continued speaking but after a while I stopped listening. His voice faded into the background, and I seemed to have a sudden intuition into the reason for his anger. For a few moments, or maybe longer, I can't say, I thought I glimpsed the hidden meaning behind what he was saying.

Then that meaning dissolved, as suddenly as it had formed.

Many years later, I would read that compulsive gambling is an attempt to control the uncontrollable, and gives the gambler the illusion that he's the master of his own destiny. And I would recall, quite clearly, the intuition I'd had that morning.

The reason Francesco resented Gino the lawyer so much was because the poor wretch was his double, his mirror image. He couldn't bear looking in that mirror and so he destroyed him, thinking he would destroy his own fear.

They both had the same fever in their souls. Francesco, too, when he manipulated cards – and people – was chasing after the illusion that he could dominate his own destiny.

Both, in different ways, were walking on the edge of the same precipice.

And I was close behind them. Very close.

❖

We went and sat down on the terrace of a bar on the sea front where all the big Fascist-era buildings are, near the Art Gallery.

Francesco said we absolutely had to get that money back. Immediately after the game, he had paid the money he had lost. He had lost it deliberately, to that dangerous man whose face I couldn't even remember, to avoid any suspicion that the game wasn't straight. Added to that was the cost of the table, the percentage of the winnings I'd paid to the manager of the club, and so on.

First of all we had to make up those losses. *One way or another*, he said, in the neutral tone of a businessman discussing a balance sheet. But I didn't like the expression on his face as he said it. I didn't like it at all.

I had the feeling something was about to go wrong. The feeling that something – something that wasn't good – was looming. The feeling that I was close to a point of no return.

So I feebly suggested we forget about the man. We didn't really need the money, we already had more than enough. We should divide our losses and drop the subject.

He didn't like that.

He was silent for a while, his jaws clenched as if he were making an effort to contain his anger. Then, without looking at me, he started speaking in a low, tense voice. He had the icy, almost metallic tone of someone talking to a subordinate who wasn't doing his job. I went red, but I don't think he noticed.

It wasn't about the money. Not only about the money. We couldn't just let an unpaid gambling debt pass. It would arouse suspicion, there'd be rumours, one way or another, and for us it would be the beginning of the end. We *had* to get that money back. All of it.

I didn't ask the obvious question. How could there possibly be rumours, since the only person who knew was the man himself, and he certainly wouldn't be going around advertising the fact that he had paid a gambling debt of millions of lire with a cheque that bounced?

I didn't ask that question because I wanted him to stop using that tone. I didn't want him to be angry with me. I didn't want him to take away his approval.

So I told myself that we had no choice. He was right. We couldn't let something like that pass. It was a risk we couldn't afford to take. We had to get that money back because otherwise, I told myself, it would all be over for us. I told myself many things, in a confused attempt to convince myself.

As he spoke, and I found reasons to agree with him, my unease and anxiety subsided, to be replaced by the stupid, false but reassuring belief that I had no alternative.

So in the end I nodded my agreement, like a businessman who has been persuaded by another businessman to do something that was unpleasant but necessary.

Because it was clear, very clear, that asking him for that money wasn't going to be pleasant.

16

THE APPOINTMENT WAS at eight in the evening, in the gardens of the Piazza Cesare Battisti, opposite the central post office and the faculty of law. My faculty.

I arrived a few minutes late and Francesco was already there.

He had someone else with him.

The man's name was Piero. He was quite ordinary-looking, of medium height and medium build, about thirty-five years old, I guessed, maybe a little more. He would have looked quite unremarkable if it hadn't been for his hair. It was long, unnaturally fair and gathered into a ponytail, tied with an absurd pink elastic band. He was carrying a thick black leather shoulder bag, which had something inexplicably indecent about it.

Piero would go with me to see Gino the lawyer – he knew where he lived – and would help me to convince him to pay what he owed. Quickly and without fuss. No point in making a fuss.

Before leaving, Francesco offered to buy us an aperitif at the Caffè della Posta. The same café where, up until the previous year, I'd often dropped in for a drink after lessons or seminars, or after doing an exam.

As I drank chilled prosecco, chewed pistachios, and saw images of my past life, I felt enveloped in a sense of unreality. As if these things, and this one in particular, weren't happening to me. And, simultaneously, as if even my earlier life hadn't been mine. Caught between two feelings of emptiness that were at once nagging and dull.

We left the café and Francesco – who obviously couldn't come with us – said goodbye. He shook hands with Piero and patted me smugly on the back.

❖

We were near the courthouse. An area that was bleak by day and dangerous after dark. Piero pointed to the front entrance of a small, wretched-looking three-storey building. He told me, in dialect, that this was where the man lived. So we sat down on the bonnet of a parked car on the other side of the street and waited.

Piero worked as a male nurse at the general hospital but, he said, he only went in when they needed him. In other words, almost never. A colleague clocked in for him and the consultant never said anything. In return, whenever they needed a favour, like tracing a stolen car or something like that, they all turned to him.

He spoke in a flat voice, partly in dialect, partly in Italian, and chain-smoked Cartier cigarettes, putting them out halfway through by crushing the paper and the tobacco between the thumb and middle finger of his right hand.

Half an hour later, Gino the lawyer appeared. He was dressed in exactly the same way as the other night. The same white shirt, the same old-fashioned trousers. As he walked he smoked.

We crossed the road and intercepted him when he was almost at the front door of his building.

He saw me first and was about to smile when he noticed Piero. The smile froze on his lips.

'Good evening,' Piero said. 'Shall we go and have a coffee?'

'I really should get home. I've been out all day.'

Piero went right up to him and put a hand on his shoulder. 'Let's go and have a coffee,' he said again. In the same flat tone. Without hinting at anything, not even a threat. Gino the lawyer didn't raise any other objections, didn't resist. He seemed resigned.

We turned the corner, walked in silence to the end of the block, and then turned again. We were in a small dead-end street without shops or bars.

'Now, what happened with that cheque?'

We had stopped in front of a closed, rusty shutter, next to an unlit street lamp. Again, Piero had spoken in the same tone, so that it almost didn't sound like a question. Gino the lawyer was about to say something when he saw Piero's hand – the one free of the shoulder bag – flash in the dim light. It made a quick semicircular trajectory and struck the man's face very hard – this man who was my father's age.

It was such a hard slap that I saw Gino's head sway and his neck almost stretch with the impact. Like one of those slow motion re-plays of a boxing match, where you see glove meet chin and the boxer's head wobbles uncontrollably from side to side before he collapses to the ground with his eyes upturned.

That was when I noticed that Gino the lawyer had a bald patch, over which he brushed his hair. I hadn't paid any attention to it before, but the slap had dislodged a long lock of hair, and you could see the bald patch in the middle of his head and that lock of hair hanging, almost perpendicular, from his forehead to his nose.

I felt something like panic. But it wasn't panic at all. It was a mixture of fear, shame, and a kind of mindless, shameful elation. The kind of thing you feel when you exercise almost absolute power over another human being.

I didn't know what to do. Gino's chin was trembling, like a child's when it's about to cry and is trying desperately to hold back the tears. The lock of hair hung pathetically, looking like a false appendage.

I felt something grow quickly inside me and go through me as uncontrollably as a wave of water rushing through pipes that are too narrow.

And I hit him, too.

I slapped him, not as hard as Piero, but hard enough, and on the same side of the face.

I slapped him to stop him shaking. I slapped him out of spite. And out of anger. The kind of anger that takes hold of you when you're confronted with someone else's weakness and cowardice and you recognise – or are afraid to recognise – your own weakness and cowardice. When you're faced with someone's failure and you try to destroy the fear that sooner or later you'll fail in the same way.

I slapped him, and for a moment he had a look of astonishment in his eyes, which immediately gave way to a resigned expression, as if he thought he deserved to be hit.

Then I spoke, in order not to think about what I had just done. What I was doing. I spoke to hold back the wicked smile I could feel creeping up on me. A smile of satisfaction at what I'd been capable of doing. But I also spoke to protect him. To prevent Piero from hitting him again. One way or another, I took control of the situation.

'Why are you forcing us to do this?'

I assumed a disappointed yet understanding expression. As if he were an old friend of mine who'd betrayed my trust but I was still willing to forgive him, if only he'd let me.

With a pathetic gesture of vanity, Gino tried to put the hair back in place over his bald spot, as if to regain a modicum of dignity now that we were talking and he had to answer me.

'But I don't have the money. I'd like to give it to you, but I don't have it right now. I've had a few problems. I can try to get it, but at the moment I don't have it.'

Absurdly, I felt like saying, OK, that's fine. Sorry we had to hit you, but you know how it is, business is business – and as soon as you have the money we'll meet again. I'd say that and then go.

Instead, Piero intervened. He had been quiet up until now, surprised, I imagine, by the turn the situation had taken and my unexpected behaviour.

He said we'd talked too much. Gino had to sign some bills of exchange, ten, twelve at the most. Naturally there'd be interest to pay, for the delay and the bother. We – he said *we* – would redeem those bills of exchange at the bank and he would do well to make sure they were covered. He didn't change his tone of voice, not even when he said that if a single one of the bills wasn't covered, he'd be back to break Gino's arm.

Gino the lawyer turned to look at me. He seemed incredulous that someone like me was involved in something like this. I looked away, nodding gravely. I was playing my part. As if to say, Of course I don't like it, but if you don't behave, it's going to happen. Don't force us to do it.

Technically, I'm committing extortion.

These words formed in my mind independently of my will. I heard them and at the same time saw them written down, as if printed on a document. Or a police statement.

We stood there in silence for a few seconds.

'Let's go and get that coffee,' Piero said at last. 'That way we can sit down, do those bills of exchange and then we can all go home.'

Gino the lawyer made one final, weak objection. 'But where will we find the right documents at this hour? Everywhere's closed.'

'I brought them with me, don't worry,' Piero said, touching his indecently large shoulder bag. You had to hand it to him, he was a professional.

We went to a bar and sat down at a table, at the far end, almost in the back room. I felt dizzy and vaguely nauseous. When the coffee arrived I couldn't drink it. Piero took out his packet of Cartiers and offered it to us. Gino said, no thanks, if he didn't mind he preferred his own. Piero insisted, in his usual voice, that he take one of his. Gino did as he was told. I took one, too, but after lighting it I let it burn down without smoking it.

Gino the lawyer signed the bills of exchange, maybe ten, maybe twelve. He wrote with his head down. I looked at those pieces of paper and his hand moving to form that elegant, painfully affected writing. I couldn't take my eyes off that pale hand, and that two-lire ballpoint pen, on the greenish surface of that cheap table.

When it was all done, I stood up, took the bills of exchange, rolled them up, and put them in my trouser pocket. Then I stood there motionless, not knowing what to do or what to say. The only things that came into my mind were absurd phrases like: thanks, see you again. Or: hope to see you again when things are better. Or else: I'm sorry, but business is business and unfortunately debts have to be paid. In all these imagined phrases, I spoke to him with a degree of respect. As I would if we'd met in other circumstances. After all, he was the same age as my father.

I was about to give him my hand, as if to express a craven sympathy, when my companion spoke. My accomplice.

'Let's go.' He sounded impatient, as if he was thinking that amateurs shouldn't do the work of professionals. Or perhaps I imagined that, and he simply wanted to go. I hesitated another few seconds, then turned and walked to the door without saying anything.

When I reached the door, I turned. Gino was sitting at the back of the bar, exactly where we had left him. He had his head propped on one hand, his elbow on the table, his other arm dangling by his side. He seemed to be looking at something with a certain vague interest.

But where he was looking there was nothing but the peeling wall.

17

LAST NIGHT THE forty drops of Novalgin hadn't worked. The headache had lessened, but that dull, oppressive shadow over his eye and temple had remained. That familiar sensation, which at any moment could become a throbbing, unbearable pain.

'Can I come in, lieutenant?'

'Of course, Cardinale.' He gestured to him to sit down, picked up the packet of cigarettes – thinking as he did so that he probably shouldn't smoke with a headache – and offered him one.

'No thanks, lieutenant,' Cardinale said. 'I've quit.'

'Oh yes, you told me. What did you want to talk to me about?'

'I've been looking over the files on the assaults committed by that…maniac we're looking for.'

Chiti took the cigarette out of his mouth, without having lit it, and leaned imperceptibly towards the sergeant. 'Go on.'

'Lieutenant, I think the most important thing isn't where the assaults took place. The most important thing, in my opinion, is where the victims were coming from.'

'What do you mean?'

'The girls were all on their way home from clubs, pubs, discos, that kind of place. Two of them worked as waitresses, four – including the one two days ago – had been in these places as customers.'

'How do you know they were coming from clubs?'

'It's in their statements.'

He was right. It was in their statements and Chiti hadn't even noticed. He had read them over and over, on the lookout for similarities in the MOs, or in the meagre, practically non-existent descriptions of the attacker. He hadn't paid any attention to what had happened before. He felt a pang of envy. Cardinale had been more intelligent than him.

'Go on.'

'I think the attacker goes to these clubs. He looks around, chooses his victim, maybe a girl who isn't with anyone – I mean, not with a man, with a group of other girls – then when she leaves he follows her and…well, does his business.'

'What about the girls who work in these places?'

'The same thing, sir. He goes to the club or pub, maybe late in the evening, and eyes up the waitress or barmaid. He sits down, drinks, waits. When it's closing time he leaves, follows the girl if she doesn't have anyone to walk her home or to pick her up…'

'…and it's also possible he's been to that club several times, to choose his prey, study her habits. Right. Right.'

At this point he lit his cigarette, in spite of his headache. For a few moments, he was lost in thought, caught between his admiration for Cardinale, his envy at not having thought of it himself, and his anticipation of the work they still had to do. And there was also a small but growing sense of excitement: at last, they had a lead, or at least a valid hypothesis, something to give impetus to this sluggish investigation.

'Have the girls said which clubs they were coming from?'

'Some have, some haven't. We'd have to question them all again. See if they noticed anyone on the night of the attack, or the previous nights. A man on his own, that kind of thing.'

'Right. We'll definitely question them again. In fact let's start with the latest one. And the two friends she said she was with. We'll see them all straight away. They're the ones with the freshest memories.' He put out his cigarette, which he'd only half smoked. 'Well done, Cardinale. Well done. Let's get them in here today. Caterina Whatshername first. We can get the details of her friends from her. Well done.'

Well done, damn it, he repeated to himself, lighting another cigarette, after the sergeant had left the room.

The headache was gone.

18

CATERINA WHATSHERNAME DIDN'T remember anything else about that night. She hadn't noticed anyone unusual in the bar. Yes, it was a place she and her friends often went. No, they hadn't noticed anything unusual on the previous nights and weeks either. No, she couldn't say if she had been followed before.

Two of her friends said practically the same things.

Things didn't get off to a much better start with the fourth girl. She was pretty, with large breasts and a mischievous but not very intelligent expression. Cardinale and Pellegrini, who were taking her statement, couldn't take their eyes off her.

'Now, Signorina…'

'Call me Rossella.'

'Ah, yes, Rossella. Could you please tell us your full name and address?'

She told them and then, for the fourth time that day, Chiti asked to hear what had happened that night. Caterina and Daniela had left first because they had classes the next day. She and Cristina had stayed a while longer, drinking and chatting.

'All right, Rossella. Now I'd like you to concentrate on what happened earlier. I mean, before your friends left. Did you notice anything or anyone unusual in the club? A man on his own, someone who looked…well, different? Maybe someone you'd seen there before, another night?'

Rossella shook her head, about to say, No, no one. And then that would just be one more idea that had led nowhere, and they'd be back where they'd started. But then the girl stopped shaking her head and seemed to concentrate, as if she'd just remembered something.

'Well, there was this guy who came in…but no, it couldn't be him.'

'What do you mean? Who came in?'

'We'd been sitting there for a while, when this guy came in and sat at the bar. He was there for ten minutes and then left. But it couldn't be him.'

'Why? What do you mean?'

Rossella looked him straight in the eyes, shook her head again and paused for a moment. 'He was handsome. I can't believe he'd attack anyone. A guy like him could have any girl he wanted. He would never have followed Caterina…'

What the girl probably meant was: Someone as handsome as him would never have attacked someone like Caterina.

'Had you ever seen him before?'

'No. Definitely not. I'd definitely have remembered him if I'd seen him before. But really, I don't think…'

'Would you recognise him if you saw him again?'

Of course she would recognise him. From the way she said it, it was clear she would have liked to do more than just recognise him, she would have liked to get to know him.

Chiti got her to describe him – one metre eighty tall, light eyes, dark hair – took her statement, and then showed her the photograph album they had put together of all the men with records for that kind of crime. Even though he didn't think it very likely that this Alain Delon lookalike would have a record as a sex maniac.

And of course he didn't. With a grimace of disgust, the girl leafed quickly through that unsettling collection of faces, their features contorted either by nature, by their own inner passions, or simply by the beating-up they had received before being photographed and filed. She closed the album, pushed it away from her with an emphatic reflex, and shook her head.

For a few moments, Chiti did not move, then he said, 'Listen, Rossella, you say you remember this man well. Would you be able to describe him to our artist, so that we can put together an identikit?'

'OK. But it couldn't be—'

'Yes, I realise that. You say it's very unlikely he could be the man we're looking for. You're probably right, but it's our duty not to rule out any possibility.'

As he spoke, Chiti was thinking something else. He felt strangely excited, and if he could have translated the feeling into words, he would have said, *It could be him, it could be him, somehow it fits perfectly with something, I don't know what, but it fits. Perfectly.*

'Pellegrini, please send for...what's the name of the artist, that corporal with the moustache?'

'His name's Nitti, lieutenant. But he's not here.'

'What do you mean, he's not here? Where is he?'

'Convalescing, lieutenant. He had a motorcycle accident and broke his arm. The one he writes and draws with.' He paused. 'Maybe the police could lend us one of theirs. They have at least two at headquarters. Surely...'

'So what are you saying? We just call up Police Headquarters, tell them to give us a sketch artist to help us solve the case of these sex attacks, and they immediately say yes, of course, dear carabinieri, here's our artist, take him, and we'll leave you alone to get on with your investigation? Is that what you think they'll say?'

Pellegrini shrugged, pursing his lips. As if to say, We're in a blind alley anyway, so any idea's a good one.

But Chiti had another idea. Maybe a ridiculous one, maybe not.

In any case, it wasn't something it was easy for him to say to his men.

Why? he wondered. Because he was a little ashamed to tell his subordinates that he could draw and that he would try to do a portrait of the attacker himself.

So he simply didn't say it, but put it into practice.

'Cardinale, please fetch me some blank sheets of paper, a pencil and a rubber.'

The sergeant looked at him in silence, frowning and narrowing his eyes, as if he hadn't quite understood. Which was in fact the case.

'Well? Are you going?'

Cardinale roused himself and went out. He came back a few minutes later with paper, pencils, a rubber, and a pencil sharpener.

'Now please go out and leave me with the young lady.'

That was all he said. He didn't want to give them any explanations. The two men went out without a word, without even looking at each other.

He and the girl stayed there for at least an hour. When Pellegrini and Cardinale went back in, there was a portrait on the desk.

Pellegrini couldn't stop himself saying, 'Did you do this, lieutenant?'

For a long time Chiti said nothing, looking from the drawings to his subordinates' faces to the girl.

'Rossella says it looks like the man she saw twice at the club…'

The girl looked around, and was about to say something, then just nodded. She seemed very uncomfortable. There were a few more seconds of embarrassed silence.

Then Chiti thanked the girl for her time, asked her to sign the statement, and told her she could go home. If they needed her again they would call her. He himself walked her along corridors and down the stairs to the exit.

When he got back to his office, the two men were on their feet in front of the desk. They stopped talking when he came in.

'Well?'

The same embarrassed silence as before.

'Well? I think we have something to work on.'

Silence again. The two men just nodded.

Chiti was about to ask what the problem was. Because clearly there *was* a problem. But without knowing exactly why, he decided to say nothing. Instead, he sent the two of them to make photocopies of the drawing. When they came back, he told them they would have to show the photocopies to all the girls and question them again about what had happened, finding out which clubs they had been to on the nights of the assaults, checking if any of them – apart from the waitresses – had been to the same places on the previous nights. He spoke quickly, too quickly, impatient to be left alone.

'When shall we start, lieutenant?'

'Ten minutes ago. Thanks, that's all.'

And he gestured to them to go. Less politely than usual, in fact not politely at all. The two men roused themselves, saluted and left. He stayed where he was, sitting at the desk.

Alone at last with the original drawing. At last able to look at it calmly.

He looked at it for a long time, while his muscles tensed throughout his body.

What had his men seen in it? And what did he see in it?

The face of a nameless criminal psychopath, or something very similar to a self-portrait? The more he looked at that sheet of paper, the more he had the terrifying impression that he was looking at himself in a mirror.

In the end the tension became unbearable.

So he screwed up the paper, put it in his pocket, and escaped from the office.

19

NONE OF THE girls recognised the face in the drawing. On the nights when the assaults had taken place, they had all been in different clubs. None had anything to add to their original statements.

The drawings were shown around in bars and clubs. The owner of one of them said he thought he had seen the face in the drawing before, somewhere. Probably in his bar, but he couldn't be sure. They had kept insisting, but the man hadn't been able to remember anything else. He thought he'd seen him, but he couldn't say where or when. And that was it.

A few days later the seventh assault took place.

It was a Saturday night and a patrol car was sent from the operations room to the neighbourhood around the Polytechnic. An anonymous phone call had come in, telling them that a girl was sitting on a car, crying, with her clothes torn, in an obvious state of agitation.

The carabinieri patrol arrived a few seconds before a police car. The police had received an anonymous call, too. It was impossible to ascertain whether or not both calls had come from the same person.

It was the carabinieri who took the girl to casualty. Chiti arrived there almost simultaneously, accompanied by one of his men, whom he'd grabbed from among the officers on night duty in the phone tap room.

They quickly ascertained that the MO was the same. But the

assault had been more violent this time, Chiti noted, more violent and less controlled. As if the man was undergoing an evolution – maybe they should call it an *involution* – and simple assault was no longer enough for him.

The girl had been beaten for a long time before the sexual assault, and then again *after* the assault. In every other way, the sequence of events was the same. The victim was attacked from behind with a punch to the head, dragged half-conscious into the entrance hall of an old building, beaten again, forced to perform oral sex, ordered not to look up, beaten some more, ordered not to move from the spot for five minutes, and to count the seconds aloud while her attacker disappeared.

This one was no prettier than the others. She was quite thin, almost angular, with short hair and a stiff, rather masculine manner. They interrogated her in the office of the doctor on duty in casualty, and she kept her eyes half closed as she replied and turned over and over in her hands her thick, old-fashioned glasses, which had been broken during the attack.

She couldn't tell them anything about her attacker's appearance. But just like the others, she did have something to say about his voice. It was sibilant and metallic, and seemed to come from somewhere else. Those were her exact words: that it seemed to come *from somewhere else* and Chiti felt a kind of shiver down his spine.

What was new was that the girl wasn't coming from a club, a pub, a wine bar, anything like that. She'd been studying at a friend's place and was on her way home. She often went home alone. She always took the same route, and had never had any trouble. Until tonight.

'It's all right, signorina, thank you. We won't bother you any further for tonight. Tomorrow we'll phone you at home, and if you're feeling better you can come to the barracks and make a formal statement. Try to rest and if you remember anything you haven't already told us, just write it down. Sometimes a small detail can be very important to the person investigating, even though it may seem irrelevant to the person involved. Goodnight.'

Bullshit, he thought as they were on their way back to barracks, sitting silently in the car.

Bullshit from the young detective's manual. He'd been a good student, at the Academy and since. He'd read books, reports, specialised journals. But real life was different. As elusive and cruel as that piece of shit they were trying so hard to catch.

They had had an idea – to be more precise, Cardinale had had it – and it seemed as if the bastard had realised it, had known all about it. And had changed methods. No more night clubs. Now he waylaid them in the street, which made him practically impossible to find. Like a bloody wisp of smoke. Why? How had he managed to sense that they were on his trail?

Or maybe all that was bullshit, too. The man simply struck at random and after months of investigation they knew nothing.

Nothing at all.

He slowly closed his hand into a fist and hit himself on the forehead with his knuckles. Once, twice, three times, hurting himself.

The carabiniere who was driving the Alfa 33 looked at him out of the corner of his eye, but kept his eyes on the road.

20

IT WAS AUGUST and the days were all the same. The heat was heavy and unsettling. Even at night the air had an almost physical texture, like a hot, wet blanket that clung to your body.

One afternoon we were walking on the beach, close to where the fishermen pulled their boats onto dry land and sold their catch. It was about a week before the mid-August bank holiday. As usual Francesco was doing the talking. Every now and again he would pause and let me say something, although he didn't listen to a word. When he started again, he would simply pick up where he had left off, or else change the subject.

After a while, he said he thought we should take a holiday. We could take the car – mine, he said, was more suitable – and just go. Maybe we could drive all the way to Spain. We didn't need to book anything.

We would stop in two or three places along the way, or even more if we felt it. And if we felt like it, we could stop somewhere for a longer time – in France, for example. In other words, we could do whatever we liked.

I immediately said yes. With a sudden vague sense of euphoria, it occurred to me that this could be a kind of heroic farewell.

Fine, I told myself, I've had these crazy few months. I've done some incredible things. Things I never dreamed I could do. I've walked a tightrope and fortunately haven't fallen off. Now we'll have this holiday and then I'll start my new life. Which in fact will be my old life, though a little different. I've seen what it's like on the other side. I've had that experience. Soon it'll be time to go back home.

I remembered *On The Road* and that famous exchange, which I'd learned by heart a few years earlier.

We gotta go and never stop going till we get there, Dean says.

Where we going, man? Sal-Kerouac asks.

I don't know but we gotta go.

Yes, we had to go and then, at last, I would come home again. Whatever that meant.

Thinking these things made me feel good. As if I'd been running in a tough race and now was within sight of the finishing line. It was nearly over. When we came back I'd tell Francesco I'd had enough. It had been an extraordinary thing to live through this adventure with him but now, for me, it was finished. I would always be his friend, but our roads were about to diverge.

When we came back, I was sure I'd find the words and the courage to say what I had to say.

'So when are we leaving?'

Francesco smiled. It wasn't his usual controlled, innuendo-laden smile. The one that always left me feeling I didn't quite know what it meant. This was like a normal smile. And I felt a twinge of sadness. He was my friend and I'd just made up my mind to dump him. I felt guilty about it, and about the doubts I'd been having more and more frequently about him, and about the two of us.

'Tomorrow. Tomorrow morning. Let's go and pack now. I'll work out a bit of an itinerary. Come and pick me up early tomorrow morning, that way we can leave before it gets too hot. Let's say seven.'

I went home. I'd been alone there for the past few days. My parents had gone to stay on a farm belonging to some friends of theirs, over towards Ostuni. The first thing I did when I got in was look for the telephone number of those friends. I wanted to talk to Mum and Dad. I suddenly felt anxious to talk to them. Our relations had been frosty ever since that Sunday lunch, but now I had the impression the ice was starting to thaw. I wanted to tell them I was going away for a short holiday, a week, maybe a little more. I needed the break, but when I came back I would get down to my studies again. I was sorry for the way I'd behaved in the last few months. I'd been through a rough time, but it was over now. For a moment I actually thought of telling them what had really been happening to me these past few months. Then I told myself, maybe it was better not to, for the moment. Maybe later. As I dialled the number I felt a bit emotional, but light-hearted. I felt fine. Everything was going to be all right.

The telephone rang for a long time, but no one answered.

They probably hadn't got back from the seaside. My mother liked to stay on the beach after the crowds had gone and read until the sun went down. She liked bathing late in the afternoon or early in the morning. My father didn't, but he adapted.

I felt bad about it and told myself I would call again later, after I'd packed my bag.

But that took longer than I'd expected.

I took a shirt from the wardrobe in my room and put it down on the table in the living room. I don't know why I had decided to use that table, which wasn't near my room, as somewhere to lay things I was planning to pack. Then I took out two more shirts. Then I took out two different ones and put back one of the ones I'd already chosen. As I walked from my room to the living room I wondered which trousers I ought to take, and how many. Two pairs should be enough. One pair of light jeans and one of khaki trousers. Then, of course, I added another pair. A cotton sweater. Or would a sweatshirt be better? Or both? Bloody hell, it's hot in Spain, all you need is a thin cotton sweater. But which one? And what about a jacket? I'd need one if we went to a smart restaurant or a casino. But you can't put a jacket in a bag. I'd better take a proper suitcase. But Mum and

Dad had taken all the suitcases. Forget about the jacket. That was a stupid idea anyway, about going to a casino. What would we do in a casino? Though maybe I could carry the jacket and hang it up in the car. Two pairs of shoes. Or just one pair, the ones I was wearing. Ten pairs of pants. That way I wouldn't have to do any washing. No, I'd have to wash anyway, because I didn't think we'd be back in less than ten days. So should I take a box of washing powder? Don't talk rubbish, if I need it I'll buy it there, or else use the soap from the hotel to do the laundry. And what about socks? People don't usually wear socks in summer. Five pairs should be enough. But would they be enough? Should I put the trousers in first, then the shirts and sweaters and then the pants and socks? Or would the other way round be better?

After an hour, I'd only packed a few things, there was a whole load of stuff on the table, and I felt exhausted. And stupid. I stood there at the table, not knowing what to do.

Eventually I told myself I was going soft in the head. I picked up items at random and threw them in until the bag was almost full. Before I closed it, I added a dozen cassettes, and two new packs of French cards.

Now I didn't know what to do. I again tried phoning my parents, and again no one answered. I ate tuna out of a tin, along with a roll left over from the day before that tasted like rubber. I had a beer. I went and sat down on the terrace with a book, but couldn't read more than half a page. I thought of going to bed but immediately realised it was a very bad idea. I wasn't tired and it was still very hot. I'd only toss and turn between the damp sheets. The very idea of it made me feel suffocated.

So I went out. There was no one about, and the empty street seemed disturbing, almost sinister. The way places that are too familiar can sometimes be sinister, if only you look around instead of passing by as usual.

When had they boarded up that door? The building was unsafe, but I'd never noticed before. And what about the old woman who lived in a one-room apartment giving directly onto the street less than a hundred metres from our building? Where was she? She was usually sitting outside, taking the air. But that night she was nowhere to be seen and the door stood closed, like a blind, fearful eye.

I felt an unpleasant shudder that started at the back of my neck and spread through my whole body. I couldn't resist the impulse to look over my shoulder. There was no one there, but that didn't put my mind at rest. I wished my parents were in. Why weren't they answering the phone? I had a premonition that something had happened. Or maybe something was happening at that very moment. For years I would remember that evening, the stupid things I did, that sense of imminent disaster. A road accident. A heart attack. Everything gone, shattered, just when I'd decided to turn over a new leaf. I tried to recall when exactly I'd last seen my parents. It had only been a few days before, but I couldn't remember. I did remember the last time we'd talked – and quarrelled – and I didn't like it. If something bad had happened to my mother and father, I thought, or even to just one of them, I'd spend the rest of my life feeling an unbearable sense of guilt. I was on the verge of tears, and for a couple of minutes I toyed with the idea of taking the car and driving to Ostuni. I quickly changed my mind, not because it was a stupid idea, but because I didn't know exactly where the farm was, so I hadn't a clue where to go.

I had been walking for at least a quarter of an hour when I passed a man of about forty who was walking his dog, a fat, ugly mongrel. The man, in contrast, was very thin and was wearing a long-sleeved white shirt, with the collar and cuffs buttoned up. He had an expressionless face. As I passed him, I could smell the sweat on him.

I wondered what he'd been like twenty years earlier, when he was more or less the age I was now. What had he expected of the future?

Had he had dreams? Had he ever imagined he would end up walking his sad-looking mongrel, with his shirt all buttoned up, on an August night, between anonymous houses and cars parked on the pavement? When had he realised the way things were going? Had he realised? And what about me? What would I be like in twenty years' time?

As I walked along the Via Putignani I heard a car with a noisy exhaust coming down the Via Manzoni.

I told myself: if the driver of that car is a man, everything will be fine, not only the trip, but everything else, too. We reached the junction at the same time. I held my breath. The car – a Fiat Duna estate car – turned slowly into the Via Putignani.

The driver was a fat lady with gathered-up hair, wearing a t-shirt, her face exhausted by the heat. She leaned forward as she drove, as if she was going to collapse onto the wheel at any moment.

As the Duna drove away towards the centre of town, I made an effort to smile. 'Fuck your stupid prophecies, Giorgio Cipriani,' I said out loud.

There was no one to hear me.

⁂

When I got back home it was too late to try and call my parents again. I would do it the following morning, somewhere along the motorway. I went to bed, leaving the window wide open to alleviate the heat.

I tossed and turned for a long time without getting to sleep. I fell asleep as the dawn light was filtering through the cracks in the shutter, and had a dream.

I was driving along some kind of motorway, across a deserted landscape as grey and sad as a winter morning. I was anxious as I drove. I had the impression I was fleeing from something very important. Then I saw objects coming towards me from the distance, rushing towards me, faster and faster, and I realised the objects were cars and I was going in the wrong direction.

How could it have happened? How had I ended up in this situation? The motorway wasn't very wide. In fact, it got narrower and narrower as the cars approached. I didn't want to die: I still had so much to do. It couldn't really be my turn yet. Things like this happen to other people. The road wasn't a motorway any more, just a narrow lane. My movements were becoming slower and slower, and my fear stronger and stronger. I could hear a siren coming closer, piercing the air.

I didn't want to die.

Because I didn't know if there was anything after death.

The alarm clock was ringing. That was all it was. I opened my eyes. For a few seconds I lay there looking at my shoes beside the bed, still hovering between one world and the other.

Half an hour later I was outside Francesco's building, ringing his entryphone. We were on our way.

21

I DON'T REMEMBER where it was I read that during the day ghosts go into hiding. It's not even a particularly perceptive or original idea. But it's true. That morning, despite the fact that I'd had not much more than an hour's sleep, despite the nightmares, despite the ghost-filled streets I'd walked along during the night, I felt fine.

Everything seemed so simple again as I drove my BMW at a hundred and eighty kilometres an hour. I didn't feel so sure any more of the meanings I'd read into our journey the evening before. On the contrary, when I recalled all those good intentions of mine, they just made me feel uncomfortable. I didn't want to think. I could do that another time. It was a beautiful day, not too hot, and we sped along with the music blasting the interior of the car, and everything was possible. I wasn't just happy, I was euphoric. I was acutely aware of everything, as if my senses had become more powerful. Everything was very straightforward, very simple. There was something primitive about seeing the colours more intensely, hearing songs I knew very well as if for the first time, touching the wheel and the gear shift, pressing down on the pedals.

About ten o'clock we stopped at a service station. I didn't know if we were in the Abruzzi, or already in the Marches. We had two cappuccinos and two slices of lemon pie. I really don't know why I remember that so clearly. I even remember picking up the crumbs that were still on my plate after I'd finished the pie. I remember the texture of the crust and the taste of the cream as it mingled with the taste of the cappuccino.

Before we set off again, I phoned my parents, but I wasn't in the same mood I'd been in last night, and would happily have done without that call. Talking to them now would only depress me just when I was feeling so light-hearted. It would remind me that I had – or should have had – responsibilities. It would force me to think. And that was something I had no intention of doing. But obviously I had to call. I couldn't just vanish without a trace.

It went just as I'd expected. In fact, worse. Where was I going? Spain? Why hadn't I told them before? What car was I using? I remembered at that moment that they didn't know I had a car. So I told a whole lot of senseless lies and they must have known they were lies, even if they didn't know what the truth was. Again, I lost my temper because I knew I was in the wrong and was being stupid. Again, I said some nasty things. It ended as badly as it possibly could, with both of us slamming the phone down and not even saying goodbye.

It was like a shutter coming down.

'Who gives a fuck?' I said, staring as the machine spat out my phonecard. I shot a look full of hatred and contempt at a fat lady who was standing there, waiting to phone, and had obviously heard everything. She turned her head away in terror and I felt a wicked pleasure. 'Who gives a fuck?' I said again as I walked back to the car.

What happened next was all very confused. The last clear memory I have of the journey is that lemon pie and that cappuccino. We drove across Italy and the south of France almost without stopping, taking turns at the wheel. When we'd started out, we'd said we could do whatever we liked. Stop wherever we wanted, maybe somewhere by the sea, and stay there a day or two. Take it easy, in other words, because we were on holiday. But now we were on the road, it was obvious this was a stupid idea. Francesco had said he knew some people in Valencia.

Valencia became our goal. We were going to Valencia, and that was it. So now there followed a sequence of blinding sun, a sunset with the universe drowning in red light, darkness, half an hour's sleep in a service station with the windows open. A lorry driver getting out of his lorry and peeing in a bush, then belching and getting back in to have a good sleep. Cigarettes, rolls, coffee, more cigarettes, cappuccinos, service station toilets, border posts, signs in different languages. Light, half-light, darkness, light again, and that feeling of urgency driving us on. Music. Springsteen, Dire Straits, Neil Young. Plus some tapes of Francesco's: heavy metal, violent and hypnotic. The further we went, the less we talked, as if we were both intent on a mission that had to be accomplished. Except that I had no idea what the mission was.

We got to Valencia more or less a day after we'd set out. We found a room in an unlikely-looking hotel and fell asleep without even getting undressed.

Outside, the air was red hot.

22

I WOKE UP about seven in the evening, bathed in sweat. Francesco had already got up and I could hear the noise of the shower from the bathroom. The room we were in was quite simply ridiculous. The wallpaper had a pattern of horse's heads on it, the two bedspreads were different colours, and the TV was a huge black and white set from the Seventies. I stared at it for several minutes, still dazed from tiredness and a sense of strangeness. There was a curious smell, unpleasant but familiar. It took me a while to realise it was me. I didn't like noticing I stank, and as soon as Francesco came out of the bathroom, wrapped in a towel, I went in to have a wash.

We went out about eight, both looking like our old selves again.

Francesco phoned his friend. I heard him talking in a mixture of Italian, Spanish and French. What I understood from the conversation was that someone called Nicola wasn't in Valencia right now, but would be back in a few days. Francesco didn't seem surprised, and said he'd call again. There was something strange about the way he said it.

Nicola was an old friend of his, Francesco told me after putting the phone down. He was from Bari but had lived in Spain for more than two years, moving around constantly and doing *all sorts of different jobs*. End of conversation. I wasn't particularly interested in Nicola. I was wide awake, I felt good, I was hungry and we were in Spain.

After eating – Valencian paella, of course, and lots of beer – we set off for a walk around the city.

We wandered from bar to bar. All the bars were open and all of them were full. Eventually, we ended up in a garden full of little tables in the half-light, a large stand in the middle, and a lot of people, some at the tables, some standing, some sitting on the ground. A smell of dope permeated the air. We found a free table and sat down. Unlike the way it had been on the journey, we both talked, a lot. We were euphoric. We talked over each other, neither of us listening to what the other was saying. A flood of words about how free we were, how we were rebels, living outside the hypocritical rules of society. How we were looking for the meaning of things beneath the stale veneer of convention. Conventions we rejected in the name of a moral code that most people couldn't aspire to.

A flood of bullshit.

The waitress who came to our table said, Hola, but then when she heard us talking she spoke to us in Italian.

She was from Florence, or to be more precise Pontassieve, and her name was Angelica. She wasn't beautiful but she had a pleasant face. She kept looking at Francesco. She asked us where we were from. She said she'd passed through Bari on the way to Greece and had been warned to watch out for bag snatchers. She took our order, still looking at Francesco, and said she'd be right back.

'What do you think?' Francesco asked me.

'Pretty. Well, nice anyway. She has something, even though she's not beautiful. Anyway she was looking at you.'

He nodded, as if to say, of course, he'd noticed. 'Let's get friendly with her. We could wait until she finishes her shift and leave together. That way, until Nicola gets back, we have someone we know in Valencia.'

'Maybe she can recommend a better hotel than the shithole we ended up in!' I said, but he didn't reply. Clearly he didn't mind the hotel. Angelica came back with our two caipirinhas.

'How come you're working here in Spain?' Francesco asked her.

She looked around her for a moment, to make sure she wasn't needed. 'I was trying for a year to pass my university exams. I'm studying languages, but I had a few problems. So I thought I'd come to Spain for a while, to improve my Spanish and try to figure out what I want to do. How about you two?'

'I'm about to graduate in philosophy and my friend Giorgio in law. We finished our exams in July and decided to take a couple of weeks' holiday in Spain. And here we are. How late does this place stay open?'

He had lied with his usual naturalness. I didn't care. I was feeling fine and I didn't care about anything.

Angelica looked around again and saw that someone at a table on the other side of the garden was trying to attract her attention. 'It depends,' she said, in a rush. 'Two or three. It depends on how busy it is. We usually stay open as long as there are customers.' She paused for a moment, as if thinking about what to say next. 'Listen, I have to run now. If you aren't in a hurry you could wait for me. I'll be an hour at the most. You can walk me home, it's only fifteen minutes from here, and we can talk properly. I can even give you some tips on what to do in Valencia and the area round about.'

We weren't in any hurry, Francesco said, and we'd be happy to wait for her. So she went back to her work and we sat and drank. I was feeling good. The air was warm and I felt pleasantly, invincibly idle. Time didn't matter, I had no responsibilities, it was as if my ego was dissolving. Part of it was the alcohol – first beer, now stronger drinks – and part of it was this exotic atmosphere, somewhere on the edge of a strange city.

We left with Angelica an hour and a half and three caipirinhas later. I've always been good at holding my drink and so I was slightly confused, euphoric, but alert. I noticed that Angelica had not only changed, but had let her long, copper-coloured hair down. She'd also put on make-up.

We drank a couple of shots of rum in a bar that was just about to close. The owner was a friend of Angelica's. He drank with us and wouldn't accept payment.

We continued on our way. Francesco and Angelica were talking to each other now, and I was excluded. Of course. So I decided to walk a few steps behind.

I looked around, with what I think must have been an absent smile on my face. It was after three, but the streets were still full of people. Not just groups of young people, drunks, junkies, but elderly men in white shirts with short sleeves and bizarre collars, and families with children, grandfathers and dogs. We even passed two nuns. They were in full habit, walking slowly along, having a lively conversation. I stopped to watch them as they walked away. To imprint them on my mind, so that – I remember thinking clearly – the next morning, or ten years later, I wouldn't think I'd only dreamed them.

Everything was improbable, unreal, intoxicating, and quite nostalgic.

We got to Angelica's building and she asked us if we wanted to come up for a drink. What she meant was: if Francesco wanted to come up. I was too tired and drunk, I said, lying. Not too drunk, I thought, to understand the facts of life. So Angelica gave me a good-night kiss on the cheek and she and Francesco disappeared together behind that filthy wooden door.

It took me more than an hour to get back to the hotel. On the way I stopped in a couple of bars and drank a couple of rums. When I lay down, after a pee that seemed to last forever, the bed started spinning, which made me think of Galileo. The founder of the modern scientific method. Or was that Newton? It was a nuisance, but I just *had* to remember. Damn it, I was good at holding my drink, everyone said so. Who was everyone? And anyway, why did I *have* to remember?

Then, all at once, everything went black.

23

I WAS WOKEN by a loud crash from outside. I got out of bed and dragged myself to the window. My mouth felt as if it was coated with cement. I tried saying a few words – swear words – just to check that everything was in working order. Then I opened the blinds and put my head out.

Two lorries had collided. Two men stood near the point of impact, waving their hands and shifting their weight from one leg to the other. A small group of onlookers had gathered on the pavement. The two men were both tall and bulky, with identical dark cotton t-shirts stretched over bulging shoulders and stomachs. They were moving and waving their hands almost in time to one another and seemed to be following some kind of choreography. The whole scene had a crazy sense of synchronicity, a strange symmetry I couldn't figure out.

Then I realised that the two lorries were the same. The same models, the same colours – white and mauve – and the same writing on the sides. They belonged to the same haulage company, and the two men were both wearing the company's t-shirt. At that point I lost interest. I shrugged my shoulders and came back inside.

Francesco wasn't back yet, so I decided to take my time. Wash, dress, go down to breakfast, have a cigarette. It was after nine now, and if I did all those things I could kill time at least until ten. If Francesco still wasn't back by then, I'd think about what to do.

But he didn't show, and I started to feel worried. Last night's euphoria had vanished and now, in the breakfast room of that shabby hotel, I felt a mounting anxiety that was close to panic. For a few minutes I thought of packing my bag and getting out of there, alone.

Then, having regained a modicum of self-control, I asked the hotel porter for a map of Valencia, left a note for Francesco and went out.

It was very hot. The city on that scorching morning was quite different from the surreal, slightly enchanted place I'd wandered through the night before. The shops were all closed, there weren't many people in the streets, and those who were looked worn out by the heat. There was a feeling of sadness, of finality.

As I left the hotel, Valencia seemed to me like a beautiful older woman you've made love to all night and now you see in the morning. Last night, she was well dressed, made up, scented. But now, she's only just got up, her eyes are bleary with sleep, her hair looks too long, and she's wearing an old t-shirt. You'd like to be somewhere else. And she'd probably like you to be somewhere else, too.

I walked around the streets with a curious feeling of determination. The longer the day went on, and the hotter it got, the faster I walked. Aimlessly, because I had no particular goal, I didn't know the city, I hadn't even looked at the map, and I had no idea where I was going.

I passed some decrepit-looking buildings and came to a large park. An elderly lady told me, without my having asked her, that we were in the dried-up bed of a river called the Turia. The river had been diverted from its course years before, and where it had been they'd built a park.

My memories of that day of fierce sunlight in Valencia are strange and soundless. Like images in a vividly-coloured but silent film.

I walked for many hours, stopped to eat tapas and drink beer in a bar which had tables outside, with old discoloured umbrellas, then walked for quite a while longer, looking for the hotel. When I found it, I felt willing to bear its shabbiness for the sake of the air conditioning. It was noisy but it worked, whereas outside it was more than forty degrees.

When I asked the porter for the key, he told me the other *caballero* had come back and was in our room. I felt relieved.

I knocked at the door of the room, then knocked again. It was only at the third knock that I heard Francesco's voice saying something incomprehensible. A moment later, he opened the door, wearing only his pants and a black t-shirt.

He went back to the bed without a word, and sat there for a couple of minutes with his eyes half closed as if looking at something on the floor. He was gradually coming to his senses. He looked like someone who's been travelling for two days in a goods wagon. At last, he shook his head and looked up at me.

'How was it?' I asked.

'She's a real sleaze, our little Angelica. Mounts you like a horse. Maybe she'll give you a demonstration one of these days.'

I had a vaguely unpleasant feeling when he said that, but Francesco didn't give me time to identify it. Tonight, he said, we'd pick up Angelica after she finished work and drive south, to the sea. We'd get there at dawn, which was the most beautiful moment of the day. We'd bathe while the beaches were still empty, then go and look up some friends of Angelica's who owned a guesthouse with a restaurant, and then we would decide if we'd stay and sleep over, because tomorrow was Angelica's night off.

I liked the idea. In any case, Francesco wasn't asking for my opinion. He was letting me in on what he'd already decided. As usual.

'Remember to bring the cards tonight.'

It was the last thing he said before lying down on the bed and turning his back to me, ready to go to sleep again.

I didn't ask why.

24

WE LEFT VALENCIA about four in the morning. There were still people in the streets. We'd picked up Angelica from the bar, driven to her place, where she'd grabbed a small bag, and then set off.

I drove, Angelica sat next to me, and Francesco sat in the back, in the middle.

Travelling at that hour of the morning, we were heading for an encounter with the universe in all its unfamiliar splendour. We left the city as the night was coming to an end and those who had peopled it were on their way home. It was cool, so we kept the windows open and the air conditioning off. Day hadn't broken yet, but we were waiting for it, talking in hushed voices.

I felt good. I'd slept until evening, and it was already dark outside when I'd woken up. And with the darkness my bad mood had dissolved. I felt full of energy and ready for everything. Francesco, too, felt good. Immediately before we left our room, he'd done something strange.

'Are you my friend?' he had said, when we were almost at the door.

I'd hesitated to reply, not knowing if he was joking.

'Are you my friend?' he had repeated, and there was something unusual in the way he said it, something serious and almost desperate.

'What kind of question is that? Of course I'm your friend.'

He had nodded in agreement and had looked at me for another few seconds. Then he had embraced me. He had hugged me tightly and I had stood there, almost frozen, not knowing what to do.

'OK, friend, it's time to go. Have you got the cards?'

I had them, and we had gone out like two crazy, innocent rogues into the night, and the day, and whatever was waiting for us. Nothing else mattered.

❖

The sun hadn't yet risen when we got to Altea. The air had the stillness and transparency of a dream. There was no one on the beach except a very old lady in shorts and a t-shirt, with a strange-looking mongrel, huge and furry, running circles around her. Lazy little waves gently lapped the foreshore.

We all undressed without a word. I've rarely in my life felt so totally at ease as I did that dawn on a strange beach in Spain. We walked slowly into the water, all around us a sense almost of the sacred, of what was about to happen. Of infinite possibilities.

We were swimming slowly out to sea, separated from each other by a few metres, with our heads out of the water, when suddenly the universe filled with pink splendour.

The sun came out of the sea and I could feel tears mixing with the drops of water that slid down my face.

❖

After breakfast, we spread our towels on the beach, very close to the sea, and lay down. People were starting to arrive.

'Why not get out the cards?' Francesco said to me. And to Angelica, as I took the cards out of my rucksack, 'Giorgio's a brilliant magician.' The expression on his face was perfectly serious, but he was playing. He was pulling our legs, both of us in different ways. But even though I was perfectly well aware of that, I felt full of pride because of what he had said.

'Come on, show her some tricks.'

I didn't object. I didn't tell her he was my teacher. I showed her a few tricks and, damn it, I was good. Angelica was watching me, frowning slightly, looking ever more surprised.

Francesco asked me to show her the three card trick. Without a word, I took out the queen of hearts and the two black tens.

I showed her the queen. 'The winning card.' I showed her first one ten, then the other. 'The losing card.' I could feel my heart beating faster, which hadn't happened to me when I'd shown her the other tricks. I gently put down the cards face down on the towel.

'Which one's the queen?'

Angelica turned over a card. It was the ten of clubs.

'Do it again,' she said, looking me up and down. There was a tone of feigned severity in her voice, but her eyes were laughing, like a child's.

'All right. The winning card, the losing card. The quickness of the hand deceives the eye. The winning card, the losing card.'

I put down the cards. She looked at them for several seconds. She knew there was a trick to it, but her eyes told her the queen was the card on her right. That was the one she pointed to in the end. It was the ten of spades. I did the trick again, with variations, and she still didn't guess right. After getting it wrong a couple of times, she asked to turn over the other two cards as well, to make sure that I hadn't conjured away the queen of hearts.

'It's incredible. I've never seen anything like it. I thought it was something you only see in films. Fuck this, you're doing it just a few centimetres from my face.'

It was at this point that Francesco suggested we could have a bit of fun with this skill of mine. As he talked, I realised he'd had this idea in mind from the start.

We would move to another beach, a few kilometres away because someone might already have noticed us here – and the three of us would make a little money. I was about to say something, but Angelica beat me to it. It was an amusing idea, she said. I looked at Francesco and he smiled back at me. He didn't really care about whatever small change we could con out of a few suckers on a beach. He wanted to celebrate this new initiation of mine. Mine and Angelica's. There was something dark about this new game of his. It was as if he was pushing us into each other's arms, but hoped to be present when we made love. He wanted to make us do something he had decided on and he wanted to enjoy watching what happened.

I paused for a few moments, then shrugged and nodded. If the two of you really want to.

Francesco told us his plan. We would drive along the coast for a few kilometres and park near another beach. I would go ahead, find a place where there were people passing, and start to play with the cards. They would watch me from a distance. After about fifteen or twenty minutes, Francesco would come up to me and bet, or rather, pretend to bet. He would lose several times, getting conspicuously angry and drawing attention to himself. Then Angelica would arrive. By this time, there would already be a bit of an audience. I would invite her to play the game. She would bet, and win, then lose, then win again. By this point, one of the onlookers was bound to ask if he could bet, too.

Angelica gave me a brief course in street hustler's Spanish.

Carta que gana. Carta que pierde. Donde está la reina? Lo siento, ha perdido. Enhorabuena, ha ganado.

It all went as Francesco had predicted, of course. Following Angelica's directions, we came to a resort beach, full of Dutch, German and English tourists. I bought a couple of cold beers from a stand,

and went and set up my pitch at the start of the sandy path that led to the beach, in the shade of a pine. I folded my towel in two, placed it on the ground, sat down, had a few swigs of beer, lit a cigarette and started playing with the three cards, apparently unaware of the passers-by. A few people slowed down to see what I was doing. I looked up and smiled at everyone without saying a word, and they went away.

After about ten minutes, Francesco arrived. He stopped to watch me, staring at me open-mouthed like a fish. The part came naturally to me. I looked up once, then twice, then a third time. He was still there. So I stopped playing and asked him, in English, if he wanted to bet. I explained to him how the game worked, moving my hands a lot as I spoke. By now, a few people were stopping to watch. When I'd finished my explanation, he put a thousand-peseta note down in front of me, on the sand. I took an identical note out of my rucksack and placed it over his. I made sure the audience was following all this.

'*Carta que gana, carta que pierde.*' Then, moving more quickly than I needed to, I placed the cards on the ground. I hadn't used any trickery. Anyone paying reasonable attention could have said where the queen was.

Francesco looked at me like an idiot convinced that he's clever, and pointed at the wrong card. Out of the corner of my eye, I noticed the look on the face of one of the onlookers. A tall, solidly-built, pear-shaped man with thick red hair and a freckled face. He didn't understand how anyone could make a mistake about something so simple, and damn it, he'd like to bet, too.

I turned over the card Francesco had pointed to, showed it to him and the people watching, smiled, shrugged my shoulders, almost as if apologising for winning, and took the money. He indicated, partly in words, partly in gestures, that he wanted to play again. We repeated the same sequence. This time, I put the queen down in a different position, though I still wasn't playing any tricks. Once again anyone who had followed my moves with a reasonable amount of attention would have been able to point to the queen. But Francesco was wrong again. The big pear-shaped guy was getting restless. He wanted to play. He was our man.

In the meantime Angelica had arrived. By now seven or eight people had gathered to watch. A thin, slightly cross-eyed man of about thirty asked in Spanish if he could place a bet. I said yes, and as I did so felt a rush of adrenalin. This was starting to get serious. He bet, and this time I played the trick. He pointed to the wrong card and lost. He played again and lost again, three, four, maybe five times.

Now Angelica stepped forward. As far as I could tell, she spoke almost perfect Spanish. She bet. The first time, she won. Then she lost. Then won again. Then lost. And lost again. I hadn't played any tricks and the big guy was trembling. When Angelica said she had had enough, Francesco made as if to step forward again and the big guy literally pushed him aside. It was his turn. No, I thought, smiling to myself inwardly, it was *my* turn.

Things went as they were meant to. He lost. He lost. He won. He lost. He lost. And so on.

After I don't know how many games, I looked at my watch and told everyone, partly in English, partly in gestures, and partly in an imaginary Spanish which consisted of putting an 's' on the end of every word, that it was late and I had to go.

The big guy went crazy. He turned threatening. He was losing, he said, and had a right to carry on playing. I looked around, pretending to be surprised and slightly worried. Then I took all the money I'd won and put it on the sand. I looked at the big guy. Did he want to play for the whole amount? One last hand, double or nothing?

For a moment, he stood there looking perplexed, as if something like a suspicion – or a thought – had crossed his mind. Francesco butted in and said he was willing to try his luck again. That was enough to make the other guy stop thinking, if that was what he had been doing. This game was his. 'Fuck it,' he said, in English.

He counted out the money and put it down next to mine, on the sand. I watched him with a look on my face that was a mixture of embarrassment and anxiety.

I held up the cards, two in my right hand and one in my left. Once more I recited the formula and put the cards down. Then I picked them up again, all with my right hand this time, and put them down again. In the jargon of card sharks, this variation on the three card trick is called the coup de grâce. Usually it's done at the end. Which was what this was.

The card on the left was the queen. Among the onlookers silence had fallen. The big guy hesitated for a moment. There was no doubt his senses were telling him the queen was in the middle. But he hesitated. I could feel my heart beating. I watched his eyes as they moved from side to side. At last he reached out and put his hand on the card he had chosen.

The one in the middle.

I slid my finger under the card and turned it over. It was the ten of diamonds.

The onlookers broke into a babble of incomprehensible comments in various languages.

I was reaching out my hand to take the money – mine and his – when the red-haired guy fell to his knees in the cool sand, grabbed the other two cards and turned them over, one after the other. Just as Angelica had done, on the other beach. He held the queen of hearts in his hand for a few moments, looking like someone who's rushed at a door to push it open and fallen flat on his face because it was already open. Then he threw the card angrily on the sand, got up again with difficulty and walked off, swearing in a language that sounded like English, though I couldn't understand a single word.

I didn't say anything. I gathered the money, the cards, the empty beer bottles, and walked away. The crowd of onlookers dispersed, still talking about what they had just seen.

❖

We didn't stay in Altea with Angelica's friends after all, but drove off again as the sun was setting. It was already night by the time we got back to Valencia. Angelica asked us if we wanted to come up to her place for a drink or a joint. I was about to say that I'd see them to the door and then go back to the hotel, but Francesco got in first.

'Sure, we'd like that. That's OK with you, isn't it, Giorgio?'

Of course it was OK with me. So we went up.

Angelica's place was a kind of bedsit, with a little balcony looking out onto an inner courtyard and a bathroom without a door, just a dirty curtain to block the view. It was hot and smells drifted in from the courtyard. I was reminded me of those apartments in the Libertà neighbourhood, near where I lived, that gave directly onto the street. I would walk past them as a child, and from behind the curtains hear voices, noises, shouts, and smell cooking smells mixed with bleach and other things. And sometimes I would imagine that if you walked through those curtains you'd find yourself in another dimension or a parallel world.

We drank rum and smoked a few joints that Angelica had already rolled. We talked in a disconnected kind of way, the way people do at times like these. After a while, Angelica took a drag, maybe the last one, on her joint and said she wanted to pass me her smoke. I looked at her through half-closed lids, smiling stupidly. She didn't wait for my answer, stuck her mouth against mine and blew the smoke inside. I coughed. They both laughed, while I tried to put on a dignified expression. Then she stopped laughing and kissed me. Her mouth was hard and aggressive, like a thick rubber gasket. Her tongue was the same: strong and elastic.

171

After that, the scene breaks up into fragments. She kisses me again, and her hands move down to unbutton my trousers. Her mouth isn't on mine any more, but somewhere else. I'm undressed, and so is she, and she's on top of me, moving slowly. She does this thing where she contracts her groin muscles, and the sensation goes right to my brain, much more than the dope and the alcohol did. She's good, I think, very good. Just like Francesco said. Oh yes, Francesco. Where is he? I turn my head very slowly – though it's the fastest I can go – and see him. He's sitting on the floor, to my left, maybe a metre away, maybe less. He's watching us and smiling vaguely. Or maybe he's looking at something else. Angelica's still moving and I think she's touching herself as she fucks me. Then everything gets mixed up again.

Before falling asleep, or whatever that sinking feeling is, I see Angelica and Francesco. They're together, moving in slow motion. Very close. But I'm far away.

Getting further and further away.

25

I WAS WOKEN by the light, the heat, my blocked nose, and the pain in my back and neck. I'd slept on the floor. My throat was burning, and my tongue was stuck to the roof of my mouth. I had a sense of constriction, of nausea.

I hoisted myself up on my arms. Francesco and Angelica were on the bed, on the other side of the room. They were fast asleep, and I sat there for a few minutes, looking at them. Francesco was lying on his back, with his arms at his sides, looking as calm and composed as usual. He was breathing silently though his nose.

Angelica was lying huddled on her side, with one hand between her head and the pillow, facing Francesco. She reminded me of a child. Then I recalled what had happened during the night and I had to look away.

I didn't know what to do. I felt so out of place there, with the two of them sleeping, in that hot little room filled with smells I didn't want to smell. But I couldn't go. The very idea of spending another morning wandering around aimlessly in that sweltering heat, on my own, filled me with dismay.

As I sat there, thinking, Francesco opened his eyes. He didn't move. He opened his eyes and looked at me without saying anything. For a few moments I thought it was a kind of sleepwalking or something like that. He sat up on the edge of the bed.

'Good morning,' he said.

'Hi,' I replied.

'Did you make coffee?'

I looked at him. It was such a banal question, it seemed ridiculous.

'It's over there,' he said, with a touch of impatience. 'In that little cabinet between the kitchen and the washbasin.'

What was? I was about to say something, when I realised he was still talking about the coffee. He'd already spent a night here, I remembered. So I went to the cabinet – a horrible pale green object, with a few faded floral stencils on it – and took out the coffee and the coffee maker.

We drank from small chipped cups. I took one to Angelica, who had woken up at the sound of our voices and the other noises we were making. She took the cup drowsily. She looked astonished, as if she wasn't used to that kind of gesture.

I felt ashamed that I was still there, after what I vaguely remembered had happened the night before. I'd have liked to be far away. I'd have liked to disappear.

Angelica got up, completely naked, and went to the bathroom. Through the curtain that functioned as a door we could hear her having a pee. I felt as if the walls of that already small room were closing in on me.

We stayed long enough to smoke a last cigarette. When Francesco said we had to go, the relief I felt was out of all proportion.

'I'm going back to sleep,' Angelica said.

'We'll come and see you at the bar, tonight or tomorrow at the latest,' Francesco replied. 'We have to see a friend.'

Sitting on the edge of the bed, Angelica nodded listlessly and raised her hand for a moment. I had the impression she didn't give a damn what we were going to do, or not do. She looked tired, as if she'd already been through this farewell ritual many times – too many times. With the light filtering through the curtains and the already oppressive heat, the room was heavy with a sense of defeat.

'Bye,' I said from the door, in a low voice. She didn't reply. As the door closed, I saw her lie down on the bed. Then the door was shut and she was gone.

We never saw her again.

❖

'Nicola should be back today,' Francesco said as we walked downstairs. 'He may even be back already.'

We went out into the harsh sunlight. We found a phone booth and Francesco called him.

'Nicola!'

Yes, we were in Valencia. Three days now. Where the hell had he been? Yes, OK, as per the agreement. We could drop by that evening. No, why should there be any trouble? A friend, and a partner. No need to worry. OK, he'd go alone, but there was nothing to worry about. Had he ever given him any trouble? OK, OK, see you later.

He was talking about me. Why did he need to reassure Nicola about me?

'Let's go to the hotel. We'll have a rest and then I'll explain.'

What was there to explain? And what agreement was he talking about? I wondered as we flinched from the overwhelming heat, hugging the walls to salvage a few scraps of shade.

We bought rolls and croissants from a baker's shop, and cheese, ham and beer from a delicatessen, to eat in the hotel, where at least the air was cool.

And there, in the noisy, insalubrious coolness of that absurd hotel, surrounded by breadcrumbs and empty beer cans, Francesco explained to me what it was we'd come to Spain to do.

26

'COCAINE?'

Have you gone mad? I was going to add, but it sounded trite. An inadequate response to the enormity of what he'd just told me. So I just said the one word, and let it hang in the air.

'Yes. Top quality, at a very good price. We can get a kilo for forty million lire. If we sell it in Bari, just as it is, without even dividing it into doses, it'll bring in more than double that. I have someone who'll take the lot and give us ninety, maybe a hundred million.'

'And where are you going to get forty million lire?'

'I have it.'

'What do you mean, you have it? You brought forty million with you in cash, just in case we'd need a lot of spending money? Or are you planning to pay for a kilo of cocaine by cheque?'

'I have the cash.'

I looked at him for a few moments. He had the cash. In other words, he'd brought forty million lire – *at least* forty million lire – with him from Bari, across the whole of Italy, the whole of France, all the way to the east coast of Spain. In other words, he'd set off with the specific intention of coming here to Spain and buying a kilo of cocaine. That might have been the *only* reason he'd left home.

'You'd already decided before we left Bari that you were coming here to buy drugs.'

He was silent for about twenty seconds. Then he rubbed his nose with his thumb and index finger and answered the way he often did: with a question.

'What's your problem? I mean, come on, tell me, what's your problem?'

'What do you mean, what's my problem? One fine afternoon in summer you say, Let's take a holiday, we'll leave tomorrow, just like that, no particular destination in mind. I agree, and we take this fucking trip, and when we're here I discover the whole thing was planned.' I broke off, because I was finding it hard to say the words that had formed in my head. I swallowed. 'I discover the whole thing was planned as part of a drug deal. Fuck it.'

'You're right. It was wrong of me not to tell you, but I was sure you'd have said no and I wouldn't have come without you.'

'Can you swear to that?'

'Look, I was wrong not to be honest with you. But what's your problem now? I mean, are you opposed to buying drugs on moral grounds, or are you thinking of the risks?'

'Both, obviously. Do you realise what we're talking about here? We're talking about buying and selling drugs. We're talking about doing something which, if we're caught, can land us in prison for so long, I don't even want to think about it.'

'Are you opposed to the use of drugs?'

'I'm opposed to *dealing* in drugs. I'm opposed to being a person who deals in cocaine, or anything like that.'

'There are people who use cocaine. Just as there are people who smoke or drink. The two of us, for instance.'

'I've heard it all before. Tobacco and alcohol are much more le-thal than drugs, look at the statistics, the best thing to do would be to legalise it, all that kind of thing.'

'So you're opposed to it?'

'It doesn't matter. It's *illegal*. It's a *crime…*'

I broke off. I looked at Francesco. He had a strange expression on his face. We were both thinking the same thing. Or rather, I knew what he was thinking and there was no need for him to spell it out. We'd be committing a crime, but what about the crimes we'd *already* committed?

'Listen, Giorgio, let's forget for a moment whether it's a crime or not. Let's look at it another way. Imagine someone who uses cocaine regularly. Maybe he likes to offer some to his friends if he can. What he wants to avoid is going once a week to a street dealer, with all the risks that entails, and all the unpleasant aspects. What could you possibly have against someone like that? Maybe he's an artist – a painter, a theatre director, whatever – and cocaine helps him to be more creative. Or maybe he just likes it and wants to stock up so that he doesn't have to worry about it for – let's say a year. Without taking any risks and without causing anyone any trouble. Imagine someone like that.'

'What of it?'

'What's the harm in selling a kilo of cocaine to someone like that? And making a lot of money in the process? We're not doing anyone any harm. We're not talking about selling heroin to some miserable junkie who hides out in dirty alleys and mugs people to get money for his fix.'

'Just tell me one thing. Is this pure speculation, or are you telling me that, apart from planning the whole trip – without my knowledge – for the sake of a drug deal, you already had a buyer lined up? Please tell me.'

'I already told you I'm sorry. I made a mistake. You're my friend and I wanted you with me on this trip, and not just to buy coke. If you're saying I deceived you, that's all right. If you're telling me you don't trust me any more, that's all right, too. Maybe I wouldn't trust myself either, if our roles were reversed. If that's it, just say it, and that'll be the end of it.'

We both fell silent. He was right. I was furious about the fact that he'd made a fool of me. Or rather I was furious about the fact that he'd made a decision like that, practically taking it for granted that he would convince me when the time came. But the fact that he had come straight out with it like that cut the ground from under my feet. The silence lasted so long, I started to think about other things. The fact that I wanted a coffee. The fact that we had to remember to check the oil and the wheel pressure before we left.

The fact that I needed a cigarette. I immediately lit one. Francesco took my packet and took one out for himself.

'There's no harm in it,' he said. 'There's not even any risk.'

'Oh, yes, that's the best part of it. There's no risk. We just have to drive across Spain, France and the whole of Italy with a kilo of pure cocaine in our car. We just have to cross two borders full of customs officers, police, carabinieri, God knows who else. No risk.' I thought I was being sarcastic. In fact, I'd simply risen to the bait.

'It's simple. We go and get the stuff. Or rather I go and get it myself, since that jerk is trying to act like a big shot. We pack it really well and send it to Bari. We send it to a post office box, and when we get back we sell it, take the money and share it between us.'

'Why should we share if you brought all the money yourself?'

'We're sharing the risks. If anything happens when we're sending the drugs, if – which is a remote possibility – we have to ditch it, in other words if anything unexpected happens, we're partners. If we lose the consignment, you give me your quota, in other words, twenty million. If everything goes well, as I'm pretty sure it will, we deduct my forty million from what the buyer pays us, and share the profits. Fifty-fifty, as usual.'

'What if we get caught before we can send the package?'

'What if a cornice falls off a building onto our heads as we're walking along the Via Sparano on a quiet spring afternoon? Come on, why should we get caught?'

Yes, why should we get caught? Come to that, who were we

harming, if things were the way he'd said? A single, rich buyer who wanted his own supply: when you got down to it, it was his business. I lit another cigarette from the stub of the previous one, and Francesco reached out and patted me on the back as a sign of approval.

After that, we concentrated on the logistics. The cocaine came from Venezuela. Better than Colombian, Francesco said. We would put it in a shoe box and pour coffee powder all round. In case they had dogs sniffing round: it confused their sense of smell. We would put a lot of wrapping paper and packing tape round it and send it. Easy, harmless, clean.

At that moment, I was certain this wasn't Francesco's first time.

27

WE WENT OUT together at sunset. The heat was only slightly less intense. Francesco had his military rucksack with him, with forty million lire in hundred-lire and fifty-lire notes inside. We walked along together for a while, then separated. We would see each other again at the hotel, he said, later that night or next morning.

It was sure to be next morning, I thought as he vanished between the buildings in the rapidly gathering darkness.

I went back to the park where the River Turia had once flowed. I liked the idea of walking on the grass, between the trees, where there had once been water and boats. Another world.

Many years later, I would feel something similar – though much stronger – at Mont St Michel, walking in the wet sand between patches of water at low tide, peering into the distance, trying to see the sea. I imagined it would arrive suddenly. I imagined a wave forming on the horizon. A great foam-laden wave, indistinguishable from the sky and the clouds. Everyone ran away, but I stayed where I was, between sand and sky, with the mount and the fortress on my right.

Watching the wave arrive.

❖

I spent hours walking in the park. I looked at the people – boys, girls, families with children – enjoying the coolness, and a feeling of gentle melancholy came over me and I thought of childhood and holidays. I'd forgotten all about Francesco, and the cocaine, and everything that had happened in the past few days and months. It was all a long, long way away. I felt pleasantly languid. The way I used to feel at the beginning of summer when I was in junior high school. Everything was possible then, and the world was an enchanted garden, luminous and at the same time full of cool, welcoming shadows, benign secrets to be discovered.

Why was I reliving the sensations of my childhood so intensely on that August night in a strange place in Spain? It was as if I was on an island, in the midst of all that was happening.

I had something to eat, drank a few beers, smoked some cigarettes and then lay down on the grass, my hands behind my head. I looked up at the sky, trying to pick out the constellations. As usual, the only one I recognised was the Great Bear.

Without being aware of it, I fell asleep.

28

THE NEXT DAY we packed our bags, checked out of the hotel, and went and got the car out of the garage. Francesco's rucksack was on the back seat. The same one he had when he had gone out the previous evening with the money. Now the drugs were in it.

I drove, and Francesco gave me directions. We were on our way to the central post office. We would send the package from there and then quietly leave.

All very easy, all very clean. But I was dying of fear.

I was driving, and yet it seemed to me as if I had eyes at the back of my head, and I couldn't take them off that rucksack, with about ten years in prison inside it if any part of this *easy, clean* business went wrong. I was dying of fear, and Francesco was in a good mood. He made jokes, said that it had taken just four days – had we only been there four days? – to be sick to the teeth of Valencia. But next time, he said, we'd have a real holiday.

I was dying of fear.

We came to a big building which I guessed was the post office. It was big and ugly: that's all I remember about it. We drove slowly past the main entrance. Francesco told me to go round the block, and when we were at the back of the building he told me to stop.

He pulled out a brown package shaped like a shoe box, enclosed in wrapping paper and sealed with light brown tape. In black felt-tip pen he had written a box number in Bari.

Francesco handed me the package. 'Now you go in, get in the

queue, and send it. Obviously you have to use a false name for the sender. I'll wait for you in the car. As soon as you come back we'll go, and this city and its fucking heat can go to hell.'

Go in.

He'd said go in. He'd wait for me in the car.

What if they caught me? What if there were police inside, and they became suspicious and made me open the package? What would he do? What would I do?

I felt a blind fear, a real sense of panic. I'd only known terror like this once before in my life. I was three or four years old, Mum had taken me to the park, and I'd got lost. I don't remember anything about that spring afternoon except that absolute fear, the sense of being totally lost, and my desperate sobs, which continued for a long time after my mother had found me.

I don't know how long I sat there with that brown package on my knees. I'm sure Francesco knew what was happening to me. I'm sure, even though he didn't say anything and certainly didn't do anything.

I'd have liked to ask him why we didn't go into the post office together. Or else I'd have liked to tell him I'd changed my mind, and didn't want to have anything to do with any of this. Let him send the drugs on his own and keep all the money for himself.

I couldn't say a word. I couldn't even open my mouth. The silence was filled with the hum of the air conditioning.

In the end, it was Francesco who spoke. 'Go on, hurry up. Then we can get a head start on the road while it's still light.'

He sounded calm. He was telling me to hurry up and to do a simple errand, because we had to go and there was no point in wasting time.

I opened the window and took the keys mechanically from the dashboard.

'What are you doing, taking the keys? What if a policeman comes along…'

His voice was neutral, lacking in tension, almost cheerful. But I felt my blood freeze. He was telling me that if the police appeared, he had to get away.

'…and I have to move the car? We're double parked. Go on, hurry up, I'm getting pissed off here.'

I gave him the keys and got out of the car, into the heat. Petrified with fear, and powerless – I was only just starting to realise how powerless.

There was no air conditioning inside the post office, only an old, noisy fan to relieve the two disheartened-looking clerks behind the counter. There was a small queue at the window for parcels. The place smelled of people and dust and something else I couldn't make out. The person in front of me in the queue was a tall, sturdy woman in a sleeveless floral dress, with long dark hair coming out from under her armpits.

The clerks were in no hurry, and nor apparently were any of the people queuing. To pass the time, I started to make bets with myself on who would come in, or on which of the people in front of me at the two windows would get seen to first.

If the next person who comes in is a man, then everything will be fine, and I'll get away. If the little old man in my queue gets seen to first, then everything will be fine.

If the next person who comes in is a woman – by now the only person in front of me was the virago with the hairy armpits – then I'll definitely get away.

Out of the corner of my eye I saw a man in uniform come in.

The police!

I saw these words inside my head, with the exclamation mark, written in thick black felt tip on a kind of white banner. I don't know which part of my brain this image had emerged from. It looked like some crude prop from an amateur dramatic show.

It was then that I realised what the expression 'bated breath' really meant. After my first glimpse of that uniform entering the post office, I immediately looked away, and stared down at a point on the floor, between my shoes. I had the impulse to run away, but even in that moment of panic I realised that it would draw attention to me and only make things worse. Though it was quite possible the policeman hadn't come in by chance. He was there for me. There had been a tip-off, they had tailed us and had been waiting for the best moment to arrest us. Or rather, to arrest me, because I was sure Francesco would get away in my car. Any moment now, they would touch my arm and tell me to follow them.

The man in the uniform walked past me, opened a small door next to the counter and went through to the other side. He had a big leather bag over his shoulder.

A postman.

It took me another few seconds to realise that I'd been holding my breath. Now at last I could breathe.

About a quarter of an hour later, I was back in the car, puffing furiously at a cigarette, my head empty, my hands shaking uncontrollably.

THE RETURN JOURNEY was as unremitting and exhausting as the outward one.

We sped on like maniacs, taking turns without a break, going back along the road we'd driven down a few days earlier, as if rapidly spooling back through a videotape made incomprehensible by the speed.

The only thing I remember about the whole journey – which lasted maybe about thirty hours – are the sharp bends in the road and the hair-raising viaducts on the border between Italy and France. It was just before dawn. I was driving at the time. Francesco had put his seat back and was fast asleep. I was exhausted and felt as if I was going to pass out, and then we would smash through the guardrail and out into the terrible void I glimpsed beyond the asphalt and the hedges and posts. Francesco wouldn't even notice what was happening. But I would see and hear everything, right up until the last moment.

The thought of it didn't scare me, and I drove on, at a speed that was crazy on a road like that – almost never touching the brake, sometimes changing gears with the cheerful, angry roar of the engine in my ears, often coming very close to the edge of the abyss, half closing my fevered eyes and reopening them just in time to swerve smoothly a fraction of a second before it was too late.

We got back to Bari on a mild August evening, unusually cool for the time of year. One of those evenings when you realise that summer is drawing to an end, even though it's still at its height. When you're a boy and these first stirrings of autumn appear in August, you feel a particular kind of gentle melancholy.

A melancholy full of memories and nostalgia, combined with the certainty – or the illusion – that you still have all the time in the world.

The city looked the same as ever. Everything, I thought, would soon go back to normal.

Even though I didn't know what normal meant any more.

Anyway, I'd soon have a lot of money in my pocket, and that was the thought uppermost in my mind now. It made me feel dizzy, as if drunk. Of course I didn't know what I was going to do with the money, but I didn't think about that.

In the meantime, the trip, Spain, Angelica, my semiconscious walks through that unreal city, that legendary dawn by the sea, then the posting of the drugs, the smells, the lights, the noises, my fear, everything was far, far away. It seemed to have happened a long time ago, or in a dream. In fact I had to make an effort of will to convince myself that it had happened at all.

As I walked home, I thought for the first time about my parents, and the fact that I would be seeing them soon, if they were back in Bari. I hadn't called them since the morning we left, on the motorway. I thought of what they would say to me – with justification – about the fact that I'd vanished, that they had been worried about me, that they didn't recognise me any more, and so on. That gentle feeling I'd had earlier quickly faded. I felt the impulse to turn round and run away, somewhere, anywhere.

But then I told myself that I was tired, overtired in fact, and just needed to go to sleep. In my own bed. One way or another, I told myself, everything was going to be all right.

One way.

Or another.

PART THREE

I

NIGHT. ARMCHAIR. HEAT. Vague memories in the pervasive dull fog of migraine.

It was his father the general, of course, who had decided that Giorgio would become an officer in the carabinieri. Just as he had been, and his father before him. The subject had never even come up for discussion.

The years Giorgio had spent, first in military school, then in the Academy, had been like swimming underwater, holding his breath, surrounded by silent, alien creatures like fish in an aquarium.

He had never had any problem adapting to discipline. You just had to withdraw, not actually be there. It was a strategy he had learned very well, right from the time he was a child.

In the last year of officers' school he had met a girl. He had gone out with her for a few weeks and then that was it. He would find it hard, later, to remember her face, her voice. Even her name.

There hadn't been any others since.

A psychoanalyst would have said that young Giorgio had severe problems forming relationships with women. Problems of inadequacy, narcissistic wounds dating back to his childhood, deep-seated traumas.

An unresolved Oedipus complex.

Is your mother's suicide, when you're not yet nine years old, enough to explain an unresolved Oedipus complex? And what has your mother's suicide, when you're not yet nine years old, got to do with that desperate, painful need for things you can't even name, because they make you afraid at least as much as you want them?

Fear and desire are a dangerous combination.

Giorgio sensed that, in a confused kind of way. During those sleepless nights, when the migraine attacked him mercilessly. During the breaks in that anaesthesia of the soul he'd had to learn too early. To survive the silence.

Fear and desire and silence are a dangerous combination.

You can lose yourself in it.

You can go mad.

2

THE AUTOMATIC GATE moved inwards, jerkily. When it was completely open I drove in and straight down the ramp leading to the underground garage. There was a space for visitors, and I carefully parked in it.

A week had passed since we'd got back to Bari. Just when I was starting to get worried and think that Francesco had handed over the coke on his own and kept all the money for himself, the call came.

'It's on for tomorrow. Pick me up about two.'

He already had the package with him. He directed me to a residential neighbourhood: apartment blocks with gardens and garages, people with money.

'I'll go, you wait in the car. There's no point in you going, too. I trust the guy, but you never know.'

For a moment, I was disappointed. I'd have liked to be present at the handover, but Francesco was right. It was a needless risk. And maybe the customer just didn't want to be seen.

Francesco took the rucksack – the same one we'd had in Spain – and disappeared into the service lift. I stayed in the car and waited. I imagined them cutting through the wrapping with a pocket knife to check the quality of the drugs. Then I told myself that was all bullshit, the kind of thing you only see in films.

After about ten minutes, the red light came on by the service lift and I saw a rapid succession of images in my mind, like a scene from a film. The automatic doors opened slowly, only it wasn't Francesco who came out, but two men carrying big guns. They were policemen. They shouted at me to get out of the car with my hands up. They made me put my hands on the bonnet, forced me to spread my legs, and frisked me.

I had to tell them I didn't know what was going on. When they asked me about the cocaine, I would say I didn't know anything. My friend Francesco had to see someone and he'd asked me to come with him. So I'd come, that was all. What was going on? What did they want with me? My voice sounded steady enough, but I felt as if I was about to burst into tears.

The lift doors opened slowly and Francesco came out with the rucksack over his shoulder. As he walked quickly towards the car, I realised I'd been holding my breath again.

'Done,' he said, getting in. I started the car, drove back up the ramp, lowered the window and pressed the button to open the gate. As we drove out into the street, Francesco pulled me by the sleeve. I turned and saw the rucksack. It was open, and packed full of banknotes. I didn't yet know how much there was but I knew I'd never seen so much money. I felt like laughing. I felt like hugging him. It had been so bloody easy that all my doubts and fears seemed absurd. And anyway, what the fuck, we hadn't done anything wrong. If this man – whoever he was – wanted cocaine by the kilo, well, that was his business. We could do a dozen deals like this, I thought in my euphoria, make a lot of money, and then call it quits. I liked the idea. At last I had my future mapped out. Things would have a meaning, and that was a reassuring thought. It swept away every vestige of guilt. It was a concept like Zeno's last cigarette. With a certain flexibility to it. Obviously, I'd completely forgotten the resolutions I'd made before the trip. Like resuming my studies, going back to a normal life, and so on. All I could think about now was the huge amount we could make, without doing anyone any harm. We didn't have to rob banks. And we didn't have to carry on doing it for the rest of our lives. A dozen deals like this – I repeated as obsessively as a madman – and then I would think about the future. I certainly wouldn't have anything to worry about. If I wanted, I could even buy a house. I'd tell my parents I'd won the money on a horse race, or whatever. God knows how much there was in that rucksack. Nothing mattered except the money. I wanted to touch it, sink my hands into it. I was a normal 22-year-old.

❖

We went to Francesco's place to divide the money. There was ninety million. Ninety bundles of hundred-thousand-lire notes. Ninety incredible bundles.

Francesco took out his share, put it aside, and handed me the rucksack with my money in it. 'Obviously, don't put it in the bank,' he said.

'So what do we do with it?' I asked, hoping he'd suggest some way we could get a return on that money.

'Whatever you like, but don't attract attention, and make sure no one can trace it back to you. If you want to put some in the bank – let's say two million – then go ahead. If in two months' time you want to put in some more – like we did with the money from the cards – there's no problem. Just don't pay in twenty-five million in one go, because one day someone might ask you to explain where it came from.'

That was an unpleasant thought, and I dismissed it immediately. I picked up the bag, closed it carefully, and put my arms through the two straps, though not in the usual way. I put it in front of me as if I was a kangaroo. This way, I thought, it would be easier to stop anyone stealing it. I said goodbye to Francesco, who didn't reply, and left. Once I was out in the street, with my hands on the coarse material, I partly walked, partly ran.

As I'd hoped, there was no one at home. After touching the money for a long time, and even sniffing it, I hid it in the big box where I kept my Tex and Spiderman comics. It was strange to see all that money in the middle of those magazines from my childhood. Bundles of banknotes mixed in with years of forgotten fantasies. Bundles of banknotes mixed in with the threadbare relics of my past.

After a while, the image made me a little nauseous. I had to turn away, do something else.

I put my favourite cassette in my ghetto-blaster and wound the tape forward. After a bit of trial and error, I found the beginning of *Born to Run*. I pressed play and lay down on the bed as the drums started up.

> *The highway's jammed with broken heroes*
> *on a last chance power drive*
> *Everybody's out on the run tonight*
> *but there's no place left to hide*

3

THE NEXT FEW weeks were directionless. In my memory, they're like a black and white film, shot unnervingly through a dirty lens, with a few distressing long shots.

Obviously, I didn't know what to do with the money. I had much more than I could possibly spend. Every now and again I moved it to a new hiding place, for fear that my mother – or the woman who came to clean twice a week – might discover it.

Since selling the drugs and dividing the money, Francesco had vanished into thin air. He didn't phone me and I couldn't reach him at home. Occasionally, I'd go to one or other of the bars where we used to meet for a drink and a chat, hoping to see him, but he never came in.

I didn't know what to do. I'd wander around the apartment and then walk the streets, with the same sense of dissatisfaction and anxiety, like a slight, annoying fever of the soul. Sometimes I took the car and went for a drive along the motorway. Two hundred kilometres an hour on the straight stretch, playing the game of keeping my foot off the brake – just slowing down a little – as I approached the bends, overtaking on the right, taking the ramps to the motorway cafés at a crazy, homicidal speed.

At other times, I'd drive along minor roads to the sea. I'd go to a different beach each time, bathe, and then lie down on a towel, thinking I would fall asleep in the warm September sun. But I never fell asleep. After ten minutes I'd start to get restless. Before long I'd be feeling really anxious, and I'd get dressed again and walk back to the car.

Then the summer was over, and my strange excursions came to an end.

One morning, I tried calling Maria. The phone was answered by a man with a strong local accent, a hoarse voice and a rude manner. I put the receiver down immediately, wondering if he would be able to trace the call. A few days later I tried again, and this time a woman answered. I had no idea who she was.

'Maria?'

'Who is that?'

I put the phone down, and never called again.

I didn't bother pretending any more to my parents that I was studying. I glided past them like a ghost, an alien being. I was aware of their pain, a pain made all the stronger, surely, by the fact that they didn't understand what was happening. They didn't say anything to me. But there was no aggression now in that silence. Only a kind of mute, uncomprehending anguish. A sense of defeat that I couldn't bear.

In order not to have to bear it, I'd look away, fill my ears with music, barricade myself in my room, go out and wander the streets.

I couldn't even read any more. I'd start a book, and after a few pages get bored or distracted. So I'd put it aside and never pick it up again. A few days later I'd take another one and try again, but the same thing would happen, even more quickly. I soon stopped even trying.

The only thing I could read was the newspapers. At least with a newspaper, you didn't have to read it from beginning to end, you didn't have to understand what you read, you didn't have to concentrate.

In addition to that, I'd developed a morbid interest in crime reports. What you might call a professional interest. I liked to read about the arrests and trials of drug dealers. In the same kind of malicious spirit as some old people who read the obituaries and tell themselves that, yet again, it was someone else's turn.

I'd read about the sentences handed down to people who'd dealt a few grams of cocaine, and calculate how much I had risked – and avoided – for dealing a kilo. I'd feel a shudder every time, a mixture of fear and pleasure. Like someone huddling beneath the blankets, in the warmth, when it's cold and rainy outside.

One day, I read about a fight in an illegal gaming club in the Libertà neighbourhood, in which someone had been stabbed. Anxiously, I searched the article for names. I had a kind of premonition – no, more like a certainty – that Francesco had been involved. I was wrong, as always happens with premonitions, but even after I'd finished reading the item, I couldn't escape a vaguely disagreeable feeling. In some way, it was connected with Francesco and me, and what was going to happen sooner or later.

Whatever it was, it wouldn't be anything good.

There were also several scare stories about the series of sex attacks which had been taking place in Bari over the past few months. The investigators believed that all the attacks had been the work of one man. They warned women not to go out alone at night and appealed to the inhabitants for help.

I skimmed through the other pages distractedly, barely aware of what I was reading, though occasionally I'd be shaken from my mindless lethargy by a particular news item.

There's one I remember especially well.

One day, I read that Gaetano Scirea had died. The sweeper of the Italian national team that had won the 1982 World Cup in Spain. I was fifteen at the time, and I remembered following their incredible, unrepeatable progress, watching as a very average group of players had turned into the best team in the world. They were unstoppable against Argentina, Brazil, Poland and West Germany. As if Destiny itself were on their side. On *our* side. Even now, when I talk about it, I find it absurd but moving.

Scirea was thirty-six years old that September of 1989, and he'd stay that age forever. He was travelling in an old Fiat 125, on a remote, potholed motorway in the middle of Poland. The driver had made a foolhardy attempt to overtake and they had crashed into a lorry that was coming in the other direction, calm, unaware, lethal. When a man becomes champion of the world, does it occur to him that he only has a few years left? And when he gets in an old Fiat 125, on some stupid road in Poland, does it occur to him that he has only a few minutes left?

❖

I phoned Francesco many times. At first, it was always his mother who answered. With that heavy local accent of hers, that sullen old woman's voice redolent of mothballs, sadness and resentment. Francesco wasn't in. No, she didn't know when he'd be back. Could she please tell him I'd called? She'd pause needlessly, sigh, and say, Yes, she could tell him, but she didn't know when he'd be back. Who was I? Giorgio again. Goodbye – or goodnight – signora. Thank you. I never managed to finish the word *signora*, she had already hung up. So I'd repeat thank you, to myself, out loud.

I don't think she had it in for me personally. I think she had a stubborn, methodical hatred of the world. The whole world outside that apartment and its stale dust and heavy odour of sadness.

Francesco never called me back. I don't suppose his mother told him about my calls, but that wasn't important. Even if she had told him, he had other things to do during those weeks. Whatever these *other things* were, they didn't include me.

After a couple of weeks and five or six of these surreal conversations with the old lady – what was her name? I never found out – she stopped answering. Every time I called, I'd let the phone ring ten, fifteen times. But no one ever answered. It didn't matter what time it was. Once I called at seven-thirty in the morning. Another time at eleven at night. No one answered. Eventually I stopped phoning.

❖

One day – it was October by now – I met him in the street. He looked strange. He'd let his beard grow, but that wasn't what made him different. There was something not quite right about him. Maybe it was the clothes, maybe something else, I don't know. His eyes were wide open and for a few moments he looked at me as if he didn't know me. Then, suddenly, he started talking as if we'd broken off our conversation just a few moments earlier. He touched my shoulder, and squeezed my arm until it hurt.

'You see, my friend, we really, *really* have to meet and have a long talk. We've come to a major turning point in our lives. How shall I put this? We've started out on a path and we really, *really* need to see it through to the end. We need to work out a strategy to achieve our real objectives.'

In the meantime he had taken me by the arm. He walked and I let myself be pulled along. We were in the Via Sparano, surrounded by fashion boutiques, elegant ladies doing their autumn shopping, groups of young people. We made our way through the dense crowds, and as far as I was concerned, a sense of menace that was just as dense and concentrated.

'In this phase of things, our very identities are at a crossroads. We have two options. The first one is to let events determine what we will be. Like pieces of wood in a river letting the current carry them along. Is that what you want? No, of course not. The second option is to swim for ourselves. Swim against the current, with strength and determination, to achieve awareness and a true existence. You see what I'm getting at?'

I had the feeling he didn't remember my name.

No, that's not right. At that moment, I was *sure* he didn't remember my name. A sentence appeared in my mind, as if written on an old typewriter: 'He doesn't remember my name.' Then it turned into a flashing neon light. *He doesn't remember my name.* It lasted a few seconds and then vanished.

'...there is a categorical imperative, and we have to follow it *to the letter*. We have to realise our *true* natures. We have to take all that potential inside us and transform it into action.'

He continued speaking for a few minutes, at a crazy, hypnotic pace, holding me by the arm and every now and again squeezing me hard just below the elbow. Then, as abruptly as he'd started, he stopped.

'Well, my friend, I think we see eye to eye about everything. We'll meet again when we have time and work things out, come up with appropriate strategies. All the best.'

And he disappeared.

4

ONE MORNING, A SERGEANT from the drugs squad, just back in Bari after three months' temporary transfer to Calabria, saw the drawing on Pellegrini's desk.

'I know this guy. I saw him one night last year, in a gaming club. We were working undercover, trying to get that gang of drug dealers in Madonnella. He was playing poker. And losing, losing really badly, but he seemed quite calm about it, as if it wasn't his problem. I'll never forget that face. Those eyes. Hold on, I remember now. After a while, I had the impression he realised who we were. From the way he looked at us. I was with Popolizio, the guy from Altamura who got transferred, and we both had the same impression and decided to leave. We didn't go back till a few nights later, and he wasn't there any more.'

He broke off and picked up the photocopy of the drawing. He looked at it for a few moments without saying anything. 'It's him, I'm almost sure of it.' Then he turned to look at Pellegrini. 'Good drawing. Who did it?'

❖

When they entered the club, the players were trying to sweep the cards and chips off the tables, but they ignored them. Chiti turned to the sergeant from the drugs squad.

'Who's the manager?'

The sergeant made a movement with his head in the direction of a bald, dark-complexioned man of about fifty who was coming towards them.

'Now look, what the hell—'

Chiti slapped him. Hard, with the whole hand, almost calmly. It was a way of saving time.

'Carabinieri. We have to talk. If you behave, we'll leave without asking any questions about what goes on in this dump. Is there somewhere quiet we can go for five minutes?'

The bald man looked at each of them in turn. Without a word, he gestured to them to follow him.

The office they entered was filthy. The stench of cigarette smoke was even stronger here than in the gaming room. The bald man gave them a questioning look. The sergeant showed him the identikit picture, asked him if he'd ever seen this man, told him to think carefully before he answered.

He thought carefully and said yes, he had seen him, he knew him.

❖

From that moment on, things moved fast. Very fast.

Within a couple of days they had identified him. According to the local register, he lived with his widowed mother. But he was never home. There was no answer when they tried his entryphone.

They questioned people coming out of the building. Signora Carducci? She'd died about three weeks earlier. Which meant that the death certificate hadn't been registered yet, Chiti thought. The son? Did they mean Francesco? No one had seen him since his mother's death. No one knew anything. Maybe he'd gone to stay with relatives in another town. No, they didn't know that for certain, it was just a guess, they didn't even know if he had any relatives in another town. To tell the truth, they didn't know anything at all. Neither he nor his mother had ever been what you'd call talkative. In other words, they were completely in the dark.

It was at this point that Cardinale, once again, had an idea.

'Lieutenant, let's try to get in.'

'And how do you suggest we do that, Cardinale? No prosecutor's going to give us a search warrant. We don't have anything. Anything at all. Just conjecture piled on conjecture. It's quite possible this man had nothing to do with the assaults. What do we tell the prosecutor?'

'I wasn't actually thinking of a search warrant…'

'So what were you thinking of? What do we do, go along there with a crowbar and break into the apartment, and maybe some neighbour sees us and calls 113 and the police come and arrest us?'

Cardinale said nothing. Pellegrini seemed fascinated by the tops of his own shoes. Martinelli stood stock still, gazing into the distance. Chiti looked at each of them in turn, an expression of dawning awareness on his face.

'So that's it. You want to bend the rules. You want to break the door down and…'

'There's no need to break the door down,' Cardinale said. 'I have a set of keys we took off a burglar.' Then, as to justify himself, 'We arrested him for at least ten jobs. Before you came to Bari. I think he's still inside.'

'Are you telling me you took a bunch of picklocks, obviously without recording them – in other words, you *stole* them – and you're keeping them for your personal use?'

Cardinale pursed his lips, and said nothing.

Chiti was about to say something else, but then thought better of it. He took out a cigarette, lit it, and smoked the whole of it. The three men waited. Nothing stirred in the office. At last he put out the cigarette, took a deep, weary breath, propped his right cheek on his clenched fist and his elbow on the desk. Again he looked at each of them in turn.

'Tell me exactly what you want to do.

5

ONE DAY I met my sister.

I was wandering as usual through the centre of town, looking in the windows of the expensive clothes shops I'd spent money in over the past few months.

I was vaguely thinking I ought to buy a few things for autumn and winter, but the whole business of going into shops, calling the assistants, trying on clothes, choosing, seemed altogether too complicated and tiresome.

When I bumped into Alessandra I didn't recognise her, or perhaps I should say I just didn't see her. She was the one who stopped right in front of me, practically barring my way.

'Giorgio?' There was a curious tone in her voice that must have been due to more than the fact that I hadn't seen her or recognised her. Maybe it was something she saw – or *didn't* see – in my eyes.

'Alessandra.' As I said her name, it struck me I didn't know how long it had been since I'd last spoken it. Whenever it had been was lost somewhere in the mysterious depths of childhood.

She was twenty-seven, but looked a lot older. Her face was prematurely lined: she had little wrinkles at the corners of her mouth, around her eyes and on her forehead. Looking closer at her face, I noticed she even had a few thin white hairs, near the temples.

'Giorgio, why the hell are you walking like that? You look like a junkie.'

How long was it since I'd last seen her? I couldn't remember. I had no idea when both of us had last been in our parents' apartment at the same time. I wondered if it had been after my new life had already started. Probably not, I thought. It must have been before I'd begun spending time with Francesco. In other words, at least ten months earlier. That was it, she had come home at Christmas, and I hadn't seen her since. How strange, I thought. She's part of my past. She's part of the life I used to lead, before I got to know Francesco. That life seemed – was – so far away. I couldn't have said if I felt nostalgia for it, or anything else. It was just…far away.

'How are you…?' I was about to say her name again, but I felt strangely embarrassed and left the sentence hanging.

'I'm fine. And you?'

It was so weird, meeting like this, like two casual acquaintances. Because that was what we were, nothing more. How are you? Fine, and you? Oh, fine, and how about the family? Which family, mine or yours?

What was weird was that I really wanted to talk to her. It had never happened before. But I was so alone. Drifting. Just having a sister seemed strange. So I asked her if she felt like a coffee. She looked at me with an expression I couldn't categorise. It wasn't exactly surprise: it was something like surprise, but a little different. And a little sad. Then she said yes, she'd like a coffee.

We walked in silence for a couple of blocks until we came to a famous old pastry shop, full of wooden fittings and wonderful bygone smells. It was almost always empty these days, and the tea room seemed suspended in some indeterminate past.

'Is it true you've given up studying, Giorgio?'

I was stunned. How did she know I'd given up studying? Obviously, my parents had told her. But that meant that my parents and my sister were on speaking terms. And that they talked about me. I found both of these things hard to believe.

'Yes, it's true.'

'Why?'

'Did Mum tell you?'

'Both of them told me.'

We sat down at a table. They were all free, apart from one on the other side of the room, where two seventy-year-old ladies with blue rinsed hair sat smoking filter cigarettes, surrounded by bags from clothing shops.

'When did they tell you?'

'What difference does it make? What's happening to you? Are you fucking up your life?'

Was I fucking up my life?

Yes, I'd say this was an economical, maybe slightly simplistic, but basically accurate definition of the past few months.

I didn't say that, but it's what I was thinking, word for word.

'Oh, no. It's just that I've been going through…' Then I thought, no, I didn't want to talk bullshit. I'd have liked to tell her everything, but that was impossible, so I fell silent.

'In a way, I'm not surprised you stopped studying that stuff. I never thought you were cut out for law. When I was small you said you wanted to be a writer. You used to write those stories in your exercise books when you were in elementary school. I never read them, but everyone said they were very good.'

In other words, my sister had noticed that I used to write when I was a child. *Those stories* in my exercise books when I was in elementary school. I'd always thought I was completely invisible to her, and now I'd discovered that she knew a few things about me. I couldn't believe it. I felt like crying and so I passed my hand over my face, like someone who's worried but is trying to keep things under control. I signalled to the waiter. He came to our table and we ordered two coffees.

'Would you like a cigarette?' I said taking out my packet.

'No. I quit.'

'How many did you use to smoke? A lot, right?'

'Two packets a day. Sometimes more. Apart from the other crap I used to put inside me from time to time.'

I looked at her without asking the question out loud. What had she *put inside her*? Had I understood her correctly?

Yes, I'd understood her correctly. I'd understood her perfectly well. My sister had been a heroin addict – with occasional forays into other mind-altering substances – for five years. I'd never known anything about it.

'When…when did you quit?'

'The cigarettes or the crap?' Her lips were slightly pursed. There was a hint of a smile, partly bitter, partly mocking. Obviously I wanted to know when she'd quit shooting up. Actually, what I wanted to know more than anything was how, when and why she had started.

She told me a story I'd only known a part of until then. It was a common enough story. The time in London, then in Bologna and other places. The abortion, the thefts, a bit of dealing to get hold of drugs, her life with *that man* – she never said his name, and I couldn't remember it and didn't ask her – the community, and her life since. Which wasn't exactly paradise on earth. Far from it. She told me about the dull, difficult life she was leading now. She told me about her sense of failure and emptiness. About how, when things get really bad, you think how good it would be to shoot up. Just once, to get past the bad times. But of course you know it won't be just once, so, one way or another, you keep going. She told me about how you keep going, the tricks you use to keep going, her friends – she didn't have many – her work. About things that were all – or almost all – so different from the way I'd imagined them.

Now, she said, she would like to have a baby. If only she could meet a man who was worth the bother.

She did almost all the talking. I listened to her, feeling a kind of dazed tenderness.

'You're not fucking up your life the way I did, are you, Giorgio?' She stretched her left hand across the table and for a moment touched my hand.

'Giorgio?'

I was sitting there, looking down at the hand she had touched. As if a trace of her hand was still there. It was so strange.

Then I pulled myself together. 'No, no. Don't worry. I've been going through a bit of a rough time. I've been kind of mixed up. It happens, I suppose. In fact, if you get a chance to talk to Mum and Dad, please tell them. I mean, tell them you talked to me – but don't tell them I told you to talk to them – and that everything's fine. We don't communicate much at the moment, but I don't like seeing them like that. Will you do that, as a favour to me?'

She nodded, and smiled, too. She seemed relieved. Then she looked at her watch and made a face, as if to say, Damn, it's really late, when you're talking you lose track of time, I really have to go now. She didn't use those words, but that was the sense of it.

She walked around the table and before I had time to stand up she bent down and kissed me on the cheek.

'Bye, Giorgio. I'm glad I spoke to you.'

Then she turned and walked out quickly. I was alone now in the tea room. The two ladies with the blue hair and the filter cigarettes had long gone.

The place was silent and unnaturally still.

6

THEY RANG THE bell by the entryphone. Once. Twice. Then a third, longer ring.

No answer.

Cardinale started trying the keys in the lock. In less than a minute, the front door opened. Martinelli and Pellegrini had stayed in the car. Chiti had said he should be the one to go in. They hadn't objected.

They climbed the stairs to the third floor, read the name on the name plate, and rang the bell.

Once. Twice. Then a third, longer ring.

No answer.

Cardinale put on latex gloves and starting working on the lock. There was a hum of machinery from somewhere. Chiti could also hear his own heartbeat and his own breathing. He tried to think what he would say if the other door on the landing opened suddenly and someone put his head out. He couldn't think of anything, so he stopped thinking. He concentrated on the hum, on his heartbeat, his breathing.

Until he heard the click of the lock. As they went in, it struck him that he had no idea how long they had been standing outside that door. Thirty seconds? Ten minutes?

Inside, it was dark and silent and smelled stuffy.

In that pitch blackness, he suddenly, for no reason, saw his mother's face. Or rather, what he assumed his mother's face was like, because he didn't remember it. Not well. Good as he was with images, whenever he made a deliberate effort to remember it, he couldn't. It was elusive, and sometimes turned into something monstrous that he had to drive out of his mind immediately.

Cardinale found the light switch.

The apartment was tidy, in a meticulous, obsessive, lifeless way. Lifeless: that was it. Chiti stopped for a moment to wonder how the apartment must have been when it was full of life.

If it had ever been full of life.

Then he roused himself, put on latex gloves and started searching. For something, anything.

There was a thick layer of dust everywhere, but no visible prints of hands or anything else. The apartment must have been unoccupied for at least a month. In other words, more or less since the mother had died. The son must have left immediately afterwards. Or, Chiti caught himself thinking for no particular reason, immediately before.

They soon came to his bedroom. In the rest of the place there was nothing interesting. Old objects, old newspapers, old utensils. All neat and tidy in a way that seemed almost ritualistic, unhealthy.

The first thing he noticed was the Jim Morrison poster. Hanging awry, the face staring out at them.

Then the Tex Willer comics, hundreds of them. He recognised some of the titles and covers. He had read them as a child.

They searched through the drawers, under the bed, on the shelves. Nothing strange or suspicious, apart from all the packs of playing cards. He wondered what they meant, and if they had any connection with the investigation, with the assaults. He really hoped this man and his cards had something to do with the crimes, and that the real culprit wasn't snug and warm somewhere, gloating in anticipation at the thought of his next assault and how he was going to outsmart all the police and carabinieri in the world.

'Look at this, lieutenant.'

Cardinale was holding a sheet of paper, typewritten on both sides.
A rental agreement for an apartment.
There was an address on the sheet.

❖

Ten minutes later, they were in the car. None of them – Pellegrini driving, Chiti beside him, the other two in the back – said a word all the way back to the barracks. As the car glided along streets made unsightly by all the cars parked with their front wheels on the pavements, Chiti thought for the first time that they were going to get him.

It wasn't a clearly articulated thought, let alone a reasoned one.

He simply thought they were going to get him.

7

ABOUT TEN DAYS after the encounter with my sister, Francesco phoned me.

What had become of me? Why hadn't I called him in all this time? Damn, we hadn't seen each other for at least two weeks. It was much longer, but I didn't tell him that. Just as I didn't tell him I'd tried to get in touch many times but he'd never been in and had never called me back.

'We really have to meet as soon as possible, my friend.'

We met about eight for an aperitif. It was November now, and cold. Two or three days earlier, hundreds of thousands of East Germans had demolished the wall and gone over to the other side, while my life had crawled along, devoid of meaning.

Francesco was euphoric, but there was a dark undertone to his euphoria that I couldn't figure out.

He took me to his favourite bar. You could see the sea from there, even when you were sitting inside. He ordered two Negronis without even asking me what I wanted, and we knocked them back as quickly as if they were glasses of orange juice, and munched on crisps, pistachios and cashews. We ordered two more Negronis and lit cigarettes.

What had I been up to? he asked me again. What had *he* been up to? I shot back. I'd tried to get hold of him many times. I'd talked to his mother. And then even she had stopped answering.

He was silent for a moment, half closing his eyes. As if he'd suddenly remembered some detail he had to tell me about before he went on.

'My mother died,' he said. There was no particular intonation in his voice. He was telling me a piece of news, without emotion. I felt my blood run cold. I tried to find something to say, some gesture to make. I'm sorry. I'm so sorry. How did it happen? *When* did it happen? How are you feeling?

I didn't say anything, didn't do anything. I didn't have time. After only a few seconds, he spoke again.

'I don't live there any more.'

'Where do you live?'

'In an apartment. I rented it a while back.'

It was the same apartment we'd gone to all those months earlier, with the two girls. He didn't remember taking me there. I was overwhelmed with a sense of anxiety that was very close to fear.

'You must see it. I'll take you tonight, show you how I've fixed the place up. But first let's have dinner.'

With the Negronis spreading through our legs and brains, we went to a rather shabby trattoria I'd never been to before. We ate a bit, but did rather more drinking. Wine and then grappa. We should start seeing each other again, Francesco said. We had to play more poker, but in style now. We'd go outside Bari, to different parts of Italy, maybe even farther afield, and make some real money. Not the small change we'd wasted our time and our talent on until now. *Our* talent, he said. *We had to start again from where we'd left off.* He repeated this several times. Apparently looking me in the face, but actually looking right through me, his gaze febrile and remote.

❖

The apartment didn't look any different from the last time, except that now there were piles of clothes on the sofa and the floor and some still unopened cardboard boxes. The place smelled of cigarette smoke, among other things. It smelled like somewhere where the windows were never opened. In fact, it smelled like his mother's apartment.

We drank more grappa, straight from a half-empty bottle without a label which Francesco fetched from the bedroom. He was talking faster than usual and, if possible, listening even less. In fact he wasn't listening at all. His eyes were wide open, staring into the distance. He took out an old vinyl disc and put it on the turntable of his expensive stereo unit. I recognised it from the first bars. *Exile on Main Street* by the Rolling Stones.

I was pretty far gone even before he went into the bedroom a second time and came back out with a white plastic packet.

I'd been pretty far gone for quite a while now.

'I kept some of the stuff from Spain. In case we needed it.'

I watched him with a stupid smile on my face as he tipped four straight lines of white powder, of identical length, onto the shiny table.

I felt a rush of fear and desire. For a moment, I lost any sense of the things around me – shapes, sounds, the concreteness of objects – and the thought crossed my mind that Francesco was gay, and that he had chosen tonight to come out. A couple of lines of coke, and then he would fuck me in the ass. For that brief moment, it seemed almost normal, or anyhow, inevitable and conclusive. A liberation, in a way.

Then, as quickly as it had come, the thought vanished and my senses started working again. I could hear the music playing and the scene in front of me came back into focus.

With one hand Francesco was rolling a fifty-thousand-lire note into a thin, straw-like tube. A simple, graceful gesture, like part of a magic trick.

He held out the tube and I took it without saying anything, but then I sat there, motionless, not knowing what to do. He made a quick gesture with his hand, as if to say, 'Go on, what are you waiting for?' But I didn't move. He took the rolled banknote from my hand, pressed his left nostril, put the straw to his right nostril, leaned down over the table and quickly sucked up one of the lines. He shook his head, pursing his lips and half closing his eyes. Then he immediately repeated the sequence on the other side, and handed the tube back to me.

For the umpteenth time, I imitated him. I did what he said. I did what he did. I sniffed hard, first on one side then on the other, and as I did it I remembered the times when I had a cold as a child and Mum would put Rinazin in my nose before I went to bed. 'Breathe in,' she would say and I would do it and immediately taste the salty, medicinal taste of the drops in my throat. The scene formed in my mind, in my *senses*, with remarkable vividness.

Then it disappeared in a puff of smoke, like something in a cartoon. I was alone again, with a slight tingling, a slight numbness, in my nose, wondering if these were the famous, amazing effects of cocaine. Francesco was sitting there, calm and composed, with his eyes half closed and his arms outstretched, his hands on the table with the palms up.

I don't know how long it was – minutes? seconds? – that I sat with my head propped on the palm of my hand. As if meditating, though I wasn't thinking of anything. Anything at all, except that cocaine wasn't all it was cracked up to be.

Then, all at once, I felt an obscenely thrilling sensation spreading through every fibre in my body, just as the first soft, down and dirty bars of *Sweet Virginia* started up. I had a very slight but inexorable tingling in my eyes. As if there were thousands of tiny pinpricks on my pupils. As if I was experiencing a transformation, like a super-hero in the comics.

It struck me that if the walls hadn't been there, I'd have been able to see for miles and miles.

I'm not sure when exactly Francesco started talking about assaulting a girl. I'm sure he did it quite naturally. Or at last, what was natural for him. He snorted a few more lines, turned the record over, lit a cigarette, drank some more grappa – and so did I – and talked about assaulting a girl. Together. The two of us.

'Doing her here isn't so much fun, when you get down to it. It's always the same ritual. You tell jokes, you make hints, just to get closer to what you both want. And she follows you, in a kind of dance, to get to what *she* wants, like a bitch on heat.'

The phrase hit me in the stomach, and I leaned forward, as if to vomit. But I didn't vomit and Francesco carried on talking. His eyes only apparently on me, but in reality somewhere else. In some nightmare country.

He carried on talking, almost without pause. He told me how exciting it could be to take a woman by force. A way of getting back to primitive roots. The rape of the Sabines. What they *really* wanted, deep down. They only realised it at the ultimate moment of pain and annihilation at the hands of the predatory male. Predatory *males*. Because the deepest form of friendship between men was taking a woman together by force. Having her together, like a ritual sacrifice.

The harmonica of *Turd on the Run* was tearing the air. The objects in that anonymous room were part of his madness. His madness, but also mine: my skin was sensitive, the smallest hairs on my body seemed to vibrate, all my senses were hyperactive, I was feeling something new and overwhelming. The sense that I was no longer bound by any rules. It was horrible, and it was beautiful. He knew that.

He told me he had been watching a girl, studying her movements. She was a student from out of town, she lived in the Carrassi neighbourhood, and worked in a pub to pay for her rent and studies in Bari. She went home from work every night, on her own, about one o'clock.

Very soon.

Francesco's mouth was moving, but the sound of his words was out of sync. And the voice was coming not from him, but from somewhere else, some indefinable point in the room.

We went out without switching off the record player. Jagger's spectral voice sounded from another world, singing *I just want to see his face*. Percussion, a distant chorus, fog.

I was going to meet my destiny. Once and for all.

8

THEY HAD HAD no difficulty identifying him, even though he'd grown a beard.

He was almost always at home during the day. He went out late in the afternoon, or in the evening, or sometimes not until night. He usually came back very late, often just before dawn.

They started to tail him immediately.

Sometimes he'd go for long, aimless walks around town.

At other times he would take his car – that strange, unreal old DS – and drive around for hours on his own, both inside and outside the city.

Sometimes he would park by the sea and stay there. They could see the glow of his cigarette in the darkness. Sometimes he'd disappear for a while. Maybe he slept, Chiti thought one night.

And sometimes they lost him – maybe he'd spotted them – and they'd give up, hoping tonight wasn't the night.

It went on like this for two weeks. Chiti – the others, too, probably – couldn't help thinking, over and over: Was it really him? Or were they wasting their time tailing someone who was clearly a bit unhinged but basically innocent? What if one evening, or one night, while they were following this man all over the city and the province, the call came in that there had been another assault?

Once, he went back to his mother's apartment, stayed there for several hours, then came out at night and again wandered the city like a werewolf.

It can't not be him, Chiti would repeat to himself. He fits, he fits perfectly. We just have to be patient and catch him as soon as he tries something.

Sometimes, Chiti thought he would like to get to know him. Go to his place and invite him out for a beer, a smoke and a chat.

He would think all these things as he sat in the car, surrounded by the smells of men, leather jackets, cigarette smoke, gun oil, pizzas and rolls and cans of beer, coffee thermoses.

Sitting in silence through the night with these hunting companions of his – sometimes he couldn't even remember their names.

Could they ever imagine the things that crossed his mind?

9

HE AND PELLEGRINI were on duty tonight. As usual, they saw him leave just after midnight.

They were about to set off after him when they realised he wasn't alone.

❈

'There are two of them,' Pellegrini said.

Chiti did not reply. This was the first time he'd had someone with him since they had started following him. He didn't like it, and at the same time it gave him a rush of excitement. He wouldn't have been able to put it into words, but there was something about them, something about the way the two men were moving, that gave him the impression they were going to *do something*.

None of the girls had ever talked about two attackers. But was there anything that ruled out the possibility?

As they let the two men walk some distance before getting out of the car and starting to tail them – not so easy at night, when the streets are deserted and there are no passers-by to mingle with – Chiti went over the girls' statements in his mind, trying to see if any of them had said anything compatible with the idea that there were two attackers. He and his men had always taken it for granted that there was just one attacker. When you think of serial crimes, you always think of a lone criminal. Maybe they'd been over-influenced by this stereotype. But what had the girls said? As he got out of the car, he wished he had all their statements to hand, so that he could check. They had all said they were struck from behind. This obviously did not rule out the possibility that there was more than one attacker.

They had all said they were dragged bodily into the entrance of a nearby building. Even that didn't contradict the possibility that there were two men acting together. In fact, when he thought about it, the theory of two attackers made this part of the act more plausible.

He had a shooting pain between his temple, forehead and eye. He tried again to gather his thoughts. What had the girls said about the actual assaults? Was there anything that would lead them to rule out categorically the idea that there were two attackers? He didn't think so, but his head was hurting more and more, and on the screen in his brain the face in the drawing grew ever larger.

The *faces* in the drawing.

Pellegrini's voice broke in on him with the impact of a stone smashing a window pane, or a mirror. Even though he was speaking in a low voice.

'We have to get going, lieutenant. They're already three blocks away. If we keep waiting there's a risk we'll lose them.'

Chiti jumped, like someone who is shaken just as he is about to fall asleep. He started moving without saying anything, his eyes on the two figures, who were already far away. Too far away, maybe.

'I'll follow them. You get another couple of cars along here as soon as possible. Our own cars, not patrol cars. Give the officers exact descriptions of the two men, and tell them to scour the area. If they spot the men they have to just keep watching them. They mustn't stop them and they mustn't be seen. And they must call us straight away. When you've finished join me.'

Without waiting for a reply, he set off, his head throbbing. Just then, the two men turned a corner, two hundred metres ahead of him. He started walking faster. He could hear Pellegrini talking over the radio, but he couldn't make out the words. Then he actually broke into a run. A few metres from the corner, he slowed down again and slowly crossed the road, as if minding his own business. He looked to his right, where the two men had turned.

The street was deserted, apart from the cars parked up on the pavements.

10

THE GIRL WAS walking quickly, and we had to hurry to keep up with her. I soon started to feel breathless. I think the effects of the cocaine and the alcohol were staring to wear off. There was a tightness in my chest, and I was finding it hard to breathe. My vision was blurred.

Francesco said the girl was about to turn into the Via Trevisani.

Just after the corner, she would pass the entrance of a disused, unsafe building. We had to stop her in front of that entrance and drag her inside. He would grab her from behind. I just had to follow him.

As the girl approached the corner, we started walking faster.

He started walking faster, and I followed.

A sentence kept bouncing around my head: 'What are you doing? What are you doing? What are you doing?' And as it bounced – bounced, like an actual physical object – between the walls of my skull, I felt a sense of inevitability. This was my destiny. Everything was about to go to hell, once and for all, and I couldn't do anything about it.

While that sentence was still bouncing around my head, Francesco put on a last burst of speed and caught up with the girl just as she came level with the entrance.

He punched her on the head, from behind. Accurately and hard. The girl didn't make a sound. Her knees bent, and she started falling. Francesco caught her before she hit the ground, and put a hand over her mouth and his other arm round her chest. He dragged her inside the entrance, saying something to her in a terrifying, sibilant voice. As if in a nightmare, I followed him.

Inside the entrance hall, there were wooden beams from wall to wall. The building was unsafe. I'd even glimpsed a sign as we went in, clearly a warning sign.

He dragged her to the other side of the hall. The place was dark and stank of cats. The girl was groaning.

'If you say a word I'll beat you to death.' Then he let go of her head and mouth. He gave her two very hard slaps, and kneed her in the side. Still from behind.

'Kneel, bitch. And keep your eyes down. If you try and look at us, I'll kill you.' Francesco's voice was unrecognisable, and at the same time familiar.

'That's enough now, Francesco,' I heard myself saying. 'Let her be.' The words had emerged of their own volition.

For a moment, everything stopped dead. Then Francesco hit the girl a few more times, in the sides, rapidly. But less accurately and less calmly than before.

He turned and came towards me. I realised I had spoken his name, and the girl had heard. She must have heard.

He punched me in the eye. It felt as if he'd pushed the eyeball through the socket into my head, and inside that empty socket there were concentric circles that grew wider and wider until they filled the whole world. There was a deafening noise inside my head. He kicked me in the groin. I bent double and he kneed me in the face. I felt my cheek tearing, over the molars. I had the salty taste of blood in my mouth. Then I vomited, a gush of liquid vomit.

I think I blacked out for a few seconds.

The rest is fragments. A film shot by a madman with an old Super-8 cine camera.

Francesco is back with the girl. He's saying something to her.

Another man staggers towards them. This other man is me, seen in a high-angle shot. From some vague point in the ceiling, amid the fetid wooden beams and rotten plaster. The two men cling to each other and there's an acrid smell. Dreamlike punches, my hands looking for his throat, his hands looking for mine, the girl's body below us as we fight. There's no longer anything human about what's happening. A bite, his flesh tearing. A scream. Like an animal's.

Then other people yelling. Francesco pulls himself away from me and tries to escape. A flashing blue light. The hall is suddenly full of people.

And then I'm on the ground, with a knee on my back and some cold iron thing aimed at a point between my jaw and my ear. Someone twists one arm behind my back, then the other, and I hear the click of metal. They drag me out, bundle me in a car, there's a noise of wheels and brakes and gears, and someone steps on the accelerator.

And we're away.

II

THE CARABINIERI STARTED beating me in the car, on the way to the barracks. I was in the back seat, with my hands cuffed behind my back, sitting between two guys who stank of cigarette smoke and sweat. The car was speeding through the city, not even slowing down at junctions, and the two men were punching me and elbowing me in the head and stomach. Calmly and methodically. This was just for starters, they said. When we got to the barracks, they'd really tear me apart. I didn't say anything. I took the blows in silence, apart from a few groans. It was strange. I could hear the sound of the blows. Dull and toneless for the blows to my stomach. A kind of amplified knocking sound when their knuckles and elbows hit my head.

I didn't say anything because I was convinced they wouldn't believe me. I was afraid. Incredibly afraid.

When we got to the barracks they kept their word. They took me to a room with nothing in it but a desk and a few chairs. There were bars on the window and, for some reason, a mirror on the wall. They made me sit on an old chair on castors, still with my hands cuffed behind my bank.

And they tore me apart, as they'd promised.

They beat me with their hands, with their feet, with the yellow pages folded in half, on my ear, and with one of those white and red sticks they use to direct traffic.

Every now and again, some would go out and others would come in. Thinking back on it, I have a feeling they were taking regular turns. Most of them were in plain clothes, though there were a few in uniform. One of the ones in uniform hit me in the face with his bandolier and cut me with the metal part.

They said it was in my own best interests to confess everything. They meant all the assaults, on all the girls. It was in my own best interests because if I didn't talk they would beat me to death and then write that I'd resisted arrest. One of them said he'd stick a funnel in my mouth and pour a demijohn of salt water down it. He was sure I'd feel like talking then.

I burst into tears, and someone hit me very hard on the side of my head.

'You piece of shit,' I heard through the fog of tears, blood and fear. Then I fainted.

I don't remember much about what happened after I came to. They stopped roughing me up, I think, or maybe they just slapped me around a little bit more. One of those who'd been with me in the car told me the other prisoners would deal with me in jail. Sex attackers aren't very popular in a place like that. At that moment I remembered my parents and my sister, and wondered how they would feel about me being in prison. It made me infinitely sad.

I think the carabinieri were about to make my arrest formal: take a statement and do all the necessary paperwork. All the time they'd been beating me up, I'd kept repeating that I didn't know anything about the other assaults. They hadn't even asked me about what had happened tonight. It didn't matter. They'd caught me in the act. They didn't need a confession.

Then the door opened, and I assumed another person was coming in to hit me. Instead, it was someone wearing a jacket and tie, who nodded to the two men who were still there. They went out and this man remained.

He was young, not much more than a boy, with light-coloured eyes. He had a Northern accent, and was quite ordinary-looking, but clean. His voice was gentle.

The first thing he did was remove my handcuffs, and I realised my shoulders were hurting, near the joint.

'Would you like a cigarette?' he said, holding out a packet of Merits. I stared at him for a moment, not sure if he was serious. Then I nodded. But I couldn't take the cigarette. My hands were shaking too much. So he took back the packet, pulled one out and handed it to me. He lit it for me and let me take three or four drags before he spoke again.

'The girl is doing well. They treated her in casualty. She's here now and we've had a chance to question her about what happened.'

He paused and looked at me, but I didn't say anything. So he carried on.

'She's in the next room. She just saw you.' He made a movement with his head and eyes towards the mirror.

I turned my head to look, then turned back to him. I didn't understand.

'Whoever's in the next room can see the people in here, without being seen.'

Just like the movies. The words appeared to me as if written in my head. That was happening more and more often.

'The girl says you didn't take part in the assault. She says you defended her.'

I moved my face a little closer to his, as if to see him better and to make sure I'd understood what he'd said. I could feel my chin trembling uncontrollably, but I didn't cry.

Thinking about it now, it seems strange, but at the time, from the moment they'd grabbed me in the entrance hall until that boy with the jacket and tie had entered the room, I'd never for a second imagined I would get out of this. I'd never for a second imagined that the girl would clear me.

It's only now, I think, that I can explain it to myself. At the time it was impossible. My sense of myself as part of these events had stopped when Francesco had suggested we assault a girl together. When he had waxed lyrical about ancestral violence and all the rest of it. The shame I felt because, for the umpteenth time, I hadn't been able to say no to him had turned me to stone inside. My guilt seemed enormous, and visible to everyone. Especially to the girl.

The fact that I had fought to defend her, out of a mixture of fear, shame and a desire for self-destruction, didn't count. I was holding fast to my guilt. My guilt for everything. That was why I hadn't even tried to say anything to the carabinieri who were roughing me up. In my own mind, I was as guilty as if I had really assaulted her.

'Why didn't you say anything?'

I half closed my eyes, and shrugged my shoulders feebly, childishly. I was starting to feel the pain from all the blows I'd taken, and I was dead tired.

He told me he was sorry for what had happened and asked me if I wanted someone to take me to casualty. I said no, and he didn't insist. In fact he seemed relieved. There wouldn't have to be a report, and no one would have to explain to the doctors, or a magistrate, how and when I had received those injuries.

'Do you feel up to making a statement? In the meantime, if you like, we can inform your family.'

I told him not to worry about my family. And yes, I did feel up to making a statement. Could I have another cigarette? Of course I could. In fact, before I made my statement, why didn't we have a cup of coffee together? Like old friends.

Soon after, a thermos arrived with two plastic cups, a packet of cigarettes just for me, and even an ice pack. The situation became almost surreal. We all had coffee together. Me, two of the men who up until a little while earlier had been beating me up – and who were now being very friendly to me – and this guy with the jacket and tie whom they called lieutenant. It was an absurd situation, but at the time it seemed quite normal.

Holding the ice pack against my left cheekbone, I told them what had happened. Part of what I said was true, part of it wasn't. I said we'd had a few beers too many and were drunk when we went out. As I said this, I was thinking that if they'd done an analysis on me they'd have found out I had more than just beer circulating in my veins, and I was pleased I'd refused the offer to go to casualty. We had seen that girl, and noticed she was on her own, and Francesco had suggested we play a practical joke on her: make her believe we were going to rape her and then, after giving her a fright, say it was all a joke and run away. We'd drunk a few beers too many, I said again, and that was why I had gone along with it, like an idiot, until I'd realised it was all getting out of hand.

They asked me about my friendship with Francesco, and if I knew anything about the other assaults. We were acquaintances rather than friends, I said. We saw each other from time to time. Sometimes we played poker together.

I don't know why I mentioned poker – I didn't have to – but it suddenly occurred to me as I was giving my statement that they'd be questioning him, too, if they hadn't already done so. What if he decided to tell them everything? For a few moments, I felt a blind, uncontrollable terror.

Did I know anything about the other assaults?

No, I didn't know anything. If they wanted my opinion – I was lying, hoping he would read my statement, would see I'd tried to help him, and wouldn't accuse me of anything – I thought it was highly unlikely he had been responsible for those assaults. They asked me what I was basing that opinion on, and I said that as far as

I knew, Francesco was a normal person.

Those were the very words I used: a normal person. Not the kind to commit that kind of act.

They told me gently – they were being gentle with me now – that I should leave personal considerations aside. They left what I'd said out of the statement.

They went back to asking me about the night's events. Did I remember the exact words Francesco had used as he was beating the girl? I hesitated. No, I was sorry but I didn't remember. It was all confused in my mind.

It wasn't true. I remembered perfectly well what he had said to her. And not just what he'd said: I also remembered the sound of his voice.

The lieutenant asked me to read over my statement. I picked up the sheet of paper, looked at the words in front of my eyes – lines, segments, curves, marks – and couldn't make head or tail of them. But in the end, I nodded as if I'd actually read it and signed with a ball point pen.

'I'll have someone see you home,' he said. Then, after a brief hesitation, 'I'm sorry for what happened.' He'd already said it once before, and he seemed sincere.

I made a vague gesture with my hand, as if to say: there's no need, these things happen. A pathetic gesture, totally out of place.

Soon afterwards, I was back in the same car they'd bundled me into, handcuffed, a few hours earlier. We drove through the deserted streets, as the darkness of night started to lose its grim but distinct colours. I was in the back seat again, but on my own this time. A young man my age was driving, and in the seat next to him was the big man who had taken down my statement. The other man addressed him as marshal. They talked among themselves about banal, everyday things.

We got to my building in a few minutes. The car stopped, and the marshal told me I could go. I gripped the door and pulled myself out with difficulty, my body aching from the blows I'd received. As I was about to walk away, he leaned out of the window.

'No hard feelings, son.' He held out his hand.

For a moment, everything was suspended. He sat there with his hand outstretched, an almost friendly smile on his fat face, and I stood between the pavement and the road, with the ice pack, the ice almost completely melted by now, against my swollen cheek.

I nodded and took his hand. It was felt flabby, and I immediately let go of it as if it were some slimy animal, or one of those sticky plastic things, made to look like vomit, that children use to play practical jokes.

Then I turned and went to the door, and they were swallowed up by the first light – liquid and ghostly – of that November morning.

12

CHITI WAS SITTING in the usual armchair. The armchair in which he sat out his sleepless nights and his headaches. The armchair in which he awoke from dreams, or nightmares, to confront the flaccid weight of another day about to begin. The armchair in which madness lay in wait for him, snarling and red-eyed like the Hound of the Baskervilles, which he had seen many years ago in a film, when he was a child.

This morning was different.

There was a strange, unfamiliar feeling of lightness as the notes of the sixth Polonaise – the *Eroica* – flowed like liquid through the silent, deserted apartment. Not at low volume, this time. The rooms, as austere as those terrifying empty rooms of his childhood, were flooded with the music and seemed to come to life. As if benign ghosts had woken and had got up to discover what was going on.

The night was coming to an end. It was like a series of scattered photos passing in front of his eyes, like something that had happened to other people. Something remote, alien.

From his pocket he took the dirty, crumpled drawing he had kept all these months. The phantom he had been hunting all these months.

He looked at it without recognising it. And the strange thing was that it had no effect on him. None at all. He couldn't see anything in it any more. Just lines that came together, moved apart, grew thicker, crossed, and disappeared. The drawing was lifeless now, the face blank, unfamiliar.

He tore the paper, once, twice, three times, four times, until the wad of torn pieces was so small and thick that he couldn't tear it any more.

Then he went and threw the pieces in the litter bin.

As he sat back down in the armchair, he thought for a moment about that young man. He felt sorry for him. He had really taken a beating, even though he had nothing to do with the crimes. Far from it. Then even this thought faded, as remote and alien as the rest of it.

He was not tired, and did not have a headache. He felt better, he thought, than he had ever felt in his life, apart perhaps from his earliest childhood, whose images, sounds, textures and smells are formed in equal parts from the material of memory and the material of fantasies and dreams.

Then he had a new thought, a painful, nagging, beautiful thought that made him feel dizzy.

He was free. Free to do many things. Free to leave. If he wanted.

Or stay. If he wanted.

Free.

Outside, opposite the barracks, day was breaking over the sea.

13

FRANCESCO DIDN'T ACCUSE me. He didn't say anything about me. He didn't say anything at all. He availed himself, as they say, of the right not to answer any questions.

Four months after that night, he stood trial for all eight assaults.

None of the victims, though, were able to identify him. One said that it *could* have been him and another that she *seemed* to recognise his voice.

The presiding judge asked her if she could be certain and she said no, she couldn't. 'It seems like his voice,' she repeated, wringing her hands, trying to drive away the ghosts.

The others couldn't really say anything at all about their assailant: his voice, his face, his general appearance.

Whoever the man was, he had always made very sure none of them saw his face.

In other words, the charges, except in the case of the last assault, were based almost entirely on the similarities in the MOs.

In an attempt to compensate for the lack of concrete evidence, the prosecutor had asked a criminologist and a psychiatrist for an expert report. Both had been asked to consider two things. The first was whether the defendant was capable of understanding and free will. The second was whether the defendant's psychological type was compatible with committing serial sexual assaults.

The two professors concluded their long report like this: *The defendant has a markedly above-average IQ (135-140) with very high scores in the field of spatial intelligence. He demonstrates manic-depressive tendencies, antisocial personality disorder with features of narcissistic disorder, a propensity towards the systematic use of lies and deceit, and a strong tendency towards manipulation in relationships. According to DSM III (Diagnostic and Statistical Manual of Mental Disorders) individuals with antisocial personality disorder find it hard to conform to the rules of society as laid down in law. They may repeatedly commit acts for which they could be arrested and systematically disregard the desires, rights and feelings of other people. They are frequently manipulative for the purpose of profit or personal pleasure. They may repeatedly lie, use false identities, simulate, swindle, or cheat at cards. Antisocal disorder, also known as sociopathy or psychopathy, does not usually imply the abolition of, or even any reduction in, the capacity to understand and exercise free will. In this particular case, the defendant, despite suffering from personality disorder, is certainly capable of understanding and exercising free will.*

The psychological portrait thus far outlined is characteristic of the perpetrators of serial crimes involving the use of violence and deception in the spheres of property and sexuality. In extreme cases, this may lead to the committing of serial homicides.

In passing sentence, the judges rejected this conclusion as insufficient. They were right, of course. It's one thing to say that someone corresponds to the psychological type of the serial sex attacker, and quite another to say that he has committed a specific series of assaults, if there is no evidence and the accusation is based entirely on conjecture. Reasonable conjecture, plausible conjecture, but still conjecture, and you don't get far in court with conjecture even if it's very reasonable.

So Francesco was found guilty only of the attempted assault on A.C.

I had to testify, of course. The night before my appearance in court I couldn't sleep, and when the usher called me I felt a wave of nausea.

I entered the courtroom and walked from the door to the witness stand with my eyes down. I answered everyone's questions – the prosecutor's, the defence counsel's, the judges' – staring constantly at a point in front of me on the grey wall. I spoke mechanically, with my back to the dock where Francesco was confined. I managed not to look his way, not even for a moment.

Leaving the courthouse, I vomited in a flower bed, in front of the statue of justice. Then I staggered quickly away. A few people looked at me for a moment, without much interest.

Francesco was sentenced to four years in prison, and the sentence was confirmed on appeal. I don't know how long he was inside. I don't know when he got out, or where he went. I don't think he stayed in Bari, but I only say that because I never saw him again.

I never heard anything about him again.

❖

For months on end, I drifted. I remember hardly anything of that time. Apart from the nausea and the waking in panic early in the morning while it was still dark.

Then, for no particular reason, I started studying again. Like an automaton. Exactly two years after that night, I graduated. Only my parents, my sister and an aunt attended my graduation. There was no party. I didn't have any friends left to invite.

Later I continued to study, like an automaton. I took the exam to become a magistrate and passed.

I'm a prosecutor now. I play my part in sending criminals to prison. For crimes like extortion, gambling, fraud, drug smuggling.

Sometimes I feel ashamed about that.

Sometimes I feel sure that something – or someone – is going to emerge from the past and suck me back in. To make me pay what I owe.

Sometimes I have a dream. It's always the same.

I'm on that beach, in Spain. It's dawn, just as it was then, and like then there's this acute feeling of a perfect moment, of overwhelming, invincible youth. I'm alone, looking at the sea, waiting. Then my friend Francesco arrives, though I can't see his face. We go into the water together. By the time we've swum out to sea I realise he's disappeared. Then suddenly I remember it's my graduation day today. I won't be able to attend, because I'm in Spain. The sky is full of dark clouds. The sun may be rising, but I can't see it. So I stay in the water as the waves start to rise, feeling that everything is ending and I can't do anything about it. Feeling an infinite nostalgia.

ANTONIA TELLS ME she's a psychiatrist. She works in a centre that specialises in helping victims of violence.

Every person chases away his own ghosts the best way they can, I think. Some succeed better than others.

She tells me she's thought of trying to find me from time to time. She never thanked me, she explains.

Not only for saving her from being assaulted that night.

But for giving her back her dignity.

I keep my head down. It isn't true, I think. I want to tell her I was a coward. I am a coward. I've always been afraid. I'll always be afraid.

Then I look her in the eyes and realise, with a shudder, that in some strange way she's right.

So I say nothing. And she also falls silent. But she doesn't go. I'd like to thank her, too, but I can't.

So we just sit there in the bar. The silence hanging between us.

Outside, it's cold.